I0684439

Legends Mate
A Wiccan Haus Novel

By
Jennifer W. Smith

Legends Mate
Copyright 2017 by Jennifer W. Smith
ISBN 978-1-68361-192-9
Cover art by Fantasia Frog Designs

Published by Decadent Publishing Company, LLC
Look for us online at:
www.decadentpublishing.com

Dear Reader,

Welcome to the Wiccan Haus. Thanks so much for selecting Legends Mate. In this story I've brought together two unlikely urban legends, Sasquatch and Siren. Though these characters stray from the typically told legends, I hope you'll enjoy Nate and Luna's exciting and sexy tale set on the mysterious Wiccan Haus Island.

The moment I discovered the Wiccan Haus stories I knew one of my characters, Luna, could benefit from a visit to the island. Luna is originally from The Vanishing Pearl: Book 3 in the Broken Water Series which is my romance and fantasy novel series based on the New England seacoast and the realm beyond. This deadly siren can be mean and spiteful, yet she has redeeming qualities. I've enjoyed writing about her deep inner struggles, challenging her resolve, and giving her something to yearn for. I hope you like it to.

To contact me or for more information about me, my novels, videos and blogs check out my website: www.jenniferwsmith.com

All the best,
Jennifer W. Smith

Wiccan Haus Order of Books

Coming Soon

Turning the Tide by Afton Locke

Welcome to the Wiccan Haus

Something wiccan this way comes to a mystical mysterious island where authors get to play and bring their love stories to life. At the Wiccan Haus you will meet Rekkus, Cyrus, Sage, Sarka, Cemil and Myron, all of whom return in most if not all the stories. Yes each one will eventually get their HEA as well.

We hope you enjoy the stories from all the authors and return time and again to keep up with the staff and meet new characters along the way. But fear not if this is your first or twenty-first story each book stands on its own. If you want to know more about the series please sign up for our newsletter.

http://thewiccanhaus.blogspot.com/p/contact-us.html

Legends Mate

Scorned siren, Luna, seeks to heal her broken heart on the mystical Wiccan Haus Island, but she doesn't have a reservation. So, she sneaks onto the island, hoping they'll let her stay and rent a room. But there has been an assassination threat against one of the Wiccan Haus owners, and Luna's unscheduled arrival makes her a prime suspect.

Nate, a Sasquatch working for the Para-Elite Force, has come to the private island undercover, posing as a guest. He must flush out the assassin. When he's assigned to trail the hauntingly beautiful siren, everything goes sideways, and Nate is shaken to his core with yearning and desire. His soul mate could be the assassin, and he may have to choose between duty and love.

Chapter One

The highest tides on earth occur in the Bay of Fundy. Strong currents created by these tides keep the waters well mixed. This increases the availability of nutrients that aid in fish population, historically deeming it one of the most productive fishing grounds in the world.

A mermaid's delight.

For weeks, Luna swam the Gulf of Maine's southern boundary in the cold waters around Georges Bank enjoying the haddock, cod, halibut, flounder, and lobster thriving there. She delighted in maneuvering the strong tidal currents into the icy waters of the Bay of Fundy.

The sun glinted off the deep-blue sea, its reflections winking like floating diamonds, and the breaking waves were white as a harp seal's fur. Luna sat on the rocky cliffs. Below her, waves crashed against the coastline, molding and altering it with a daily fifty-two-foot tidal range. The scenery around her offered a rugged and beautiful combination, but she failed to enjoy it. Sad and wandering thoughts left her adrift.

The wind shifted, and strands of dark hair slapped across her face. Annoyed, she brushed it away. Luna realized she'd sat long enough for her waist-long hair to dry—completely. Returning to the water wouldn't comfort her. Though she'd been the one to leave her previous situation—a lover cast aside—this loneliness and isolation made her desperate to find a new life. She couldn't return. And she'd stalled, swimming the open sea long enough. A destination loomed in her mind.

In the region not far from where she sat was an island—not just any island—but one she'd heard about through hushed tones. It was said the island housed a secluded resort for guests both human and nonhuman. The Wiccan Haus, run by four mystical siblings, was a distinguished place of healing and regeneration. *Can the Wiccan Haus and its magic help heal my trampled heart? Many suffered from a broken heart, but surely mine resulted in the cruelest twist of fate.*

Riding out with the tide, Luna recalled her adolescent years when the water god discovered her. The moment the water god heard her singing voice, he had swiftly and passionately deemed her *his*.

She swam faster as she remembered his touch—

allowing the memories to ease her sorrow—if only for a little while.

To distinguish her from the others of her kind, the god had immediately given her the ability to walk on land. Her species of female water natives were called sirens by the land-dwellers of her realm because similarly their songs lured victims into the water. Though these distinct females had no tails like the legendary sirens and mermaids of other realms, their legs were not meant to withstand long periods out of the water. This alteration the god had given Luna, to walk on land, had lent to the resentment of the other sirens of her kind, who were already of a spiteful and jealous nature. In a sense, Luna had *sisters*, but they were a fickle and untrustworthy lot. Returning to their fold after her disgrace was unappealing at best.

The water god favored all the sirens with his attention when he wanted them. However, Luna was his favored one. Not only had he physically altered her, but he'd gifted her with extended life—how could she not love him above all things?

Apparently, he didn't return her love in the same way. Just two centuries together and then he heartlessly chose another.

Luna was a siren scorned. She would never speak

his name, Suijin, again.

Though her kind came from the waters of another realm, she knew of mermaids who flourished in the human oceans. History's legends of mermaids and sirens ran close. Luna learned a mermaid from the royal family resided on the Wiccan Haus island and helped women in need, her reputation preceded her. *Could she help me?*

Staying under the water and riding the Eastern Maine Coastal Current, Luna traveled south. She broke the surface. A warm breeze caressed her face. Ahead, a wall of fog met the jewel-toned blue water.

Hmm. A security barrier. I'm in the right place. All I have to do is swim under it.

She dove deep and met resistance—there was something invisible there. The magical force went all the way to the sand, but she was agile and determined to get through it. Her limbs throbbed with discomfort infused by the enchanted magic undulating in the waters around her. It left a zinging undercurrent in her veins, but she'd made it through.

The second obstacle she faced, but outmaneuvered undetected, was the patrols. Heart racing at the thrill of dodging security, she finally broke the surface. The green oasis rose from the sea abundant in lush, green hills, and forests. Intrigued, she swam closer. Near the shore, something in the air evoked a calmness in Luna—balance and Zen buzzed on the breeze. Did guests leave here on this frequency?

During low tide, she walked onto the deserted beach. The zinging sensation, from crossing the magic barrier minutes ago, faded as she shook out her arms. She wrung out her sopping wet, black hair then adjusted the satchel hanging against her halter dress, all the while contemplating what to do next.

She glanced one last time at the fog on the horizon, and pain squeezed her chest. Heartache was a cruel bitch! *There is no turning back. I won't return to watch him put another woman before me. Not again.* She squared her narrow shoulders.

"Welcome to the Wiccan Haus," a voice rang out.

Twisting around, she gasped. Alarms rang in her head. Trespassing was a crime in the human realm, and she had infiltrated their island's defenses. Her heartbeat sped up.

A man waltzed out from behind a cluster of barnacle-studded boulders. Two more men dressed in black followed close behind him, their expressions stern and uncompromising. The poised and elegant fellow stopped, smiling like he'd been expecting her arrival. He raised his hand to stay the military twins. Though the smiling man's clothes billowed around him in a lavender cloud of fabric, it was his long, blond hair that caught Luna's attention. It was a paler shade of blond hair than the woman who had replaced her.

"Oh, hello. I don't have a reservation, but I'm interested in a room. Are there any available?" Patting the satchel at her hip, a thought suddenly occurred to her. "How much are the rooms?" She visited the human realm often enough to know about currency. The water god had accumulated vast wealth and riches to generate payment for whatever he required. She'd taken money with her before she left but now questioned if she'd taken enough.

The man's icy-blues gazed on her with kindness. "Wiccan Haus is here for those who need it. What is your name?"

"Luna."

"Luna." He rolled the name on his tongue and smiled.

The water god had given her the name. It meant the moon. He'd said her songs drew him to her like the moon's pull on the tides. Years later, he'd taught her about the other creatures of the land and how the moon called to shifters, changelings, and creatures of the night. She wondered if she would meet any of those kind here on the island.

It seemed the man surmised she wasn't human. Could he detect she was a siren? Siren's from her realm had distinct traits; their large eyes and youthful beauty were a hauntingly accurate sign of their identity.

"Luna, I'm Cemil, it's nice to make your acquaintance. My three siblings, Cyrus, Sarka, Sage, and I own and operate the Wiccan Haus. Let's see about getting you a room." He offered her his arm with a flourish. She folded her small hand into the solid bend of his elbow.

She glanced over her shoulder at the comforting, undulating sea blanket. It was time to move on and put the water god in her past. She turned away from the waves. The military twins fell into step behind them.

"If you don't mind, we'll take the hill path and stroll by the lake," Cemil said. "This island supports a colony of bungalows and a main lodge. I'm certain you will want to spend time at the lake while you are here this week—we book a week at a time. And do not worry about anything; the Wiccan Haus will provide everything you need."

She nodded, while contemplating the strangely

perfect world around her—her amiable companion, the lush grass, and the perfectly blue sky. "I've heard this is a place of spiritual and emotional healing. How does one heal here exactly?" Could magic be involved? What could she expect?

"It is true. Many have found what they seek or found what they didn't even know they were looking for."

His gaze dropped to hers. She was thankful he didn't ask why she was here.

"But *how*, you ask. Well, we have wonderful therapies like yoga, acupressure, fire cupping, hydrotherapy...just to name a few. In fact, you should consider taking one of Selena's classes. I think the two of you would get along famously." He acted out the last word with an exaggerated wave of his hand, pulling it into a fist. "Also, we do ask everyone attends dinner. It's mandatory actually. As a result, you'll get a chance to meet some interesting guests and make some friends."

"Dinner?" she repeated weakly. *With humans!* How was she supposed to stomach cooked meats and baked grains?

"Do you like sushi? We have the freshest on the island."

Did he read my mind? "Yes, it's my favorite."

His voice raised a notch. "One of my sisters, Sage, is an herbalist who knows just what everyone needs to nourish their souls and their stomachs. So she can make you a shake tailored just for you. I highly recommend her service." He smiled brightly, but his pale eyes reflected amusement as if he hid a secret.

"I'm a bit of an herbalist myself. I look forward to meeting your sister Sage." Of course, Luna used underwater ingredients.

At the crest of the hill, the waters of a lake sparkled through the trees.

"Did I mention it's a saltwater lake?"

"No, but that's perfect." She smiled at his pointedness. He seemed to know she was a being from the sea.

While they continued down the path, the acute presence of the security men behind her, and the gravel crunching under their boots, grated on her nerves. She refocused on her companion's words.

"Other guests are arriving today. The ferry from the mainland should be unloaded by now."

Within ten minutes, the Wiccan Haus came into view. The steep roofline of the half-timbered building stirred to life a century-old memory. The water god

9

had taken her to a holiday festival in Germany to sample some spirits. They'd walked among humans as she was about to do now. She despised humans—as they despised sirens. The races were enemies from the start of creation. She'd felt completely safe walking in the crowds beside a god. But, now, she earnestly questioned if this was worth the risk, being outnumbered. *A ferry from the mainland meant how many humans?* The water god had warned her of the existence of others and told her stories of other beings and realms, but she'd never experienced anything more foreign than humans.

"It's a charming house. How many humans—I mean—guests stay?"

Cemil patted the hand she rested at his elbow. "The ferry holds twelve—mostly humans. The other twelve arrive through the portal. Don't worry, there's room for you." He let go of her hand, stepping out of her reach. "Follow me."

Only a few people lingered outside. They were holding their devices in the air, looking puzzled.

Cemil grimaced. "If you will excuse me, Luna, I must inform the new guests their phones don't work on this island. Some get positively ugly." Before he took a step farther, he stopped and held up a finger at

Luna and the men who stood adjacent waiting for further instruction. "Speaking of disappointing news...there is one requirement."

She tightened her grip on the satchel's strap.

"You will need to refrain from singing *and* humming around the guests. In fact, you'll need to sign a contract."

He knows I'm a siren.

She nodded, embarrassed by his implication. Sirens only sang to lure their target into submission— and kill them.

"Splendid. You go on inside and check in at the reception desk with Myron while I speak to my other guests." He turned to the men. "You're dismissed."

With curt nods, the men about-faced and retreated. Luna hesitated a moment, watching Cemil charm the newcomers, much like he'd charmed her. He'd welcomed her, knowing she was a siren.

Stepping through the entrance into a spacious lobby, Luna stopped. Confused, she tilted her head. The inside was not as she'd expected. The quaint outside of the lodge didn't match the abundant, upscale inside. Odd.

Luna approached the desk. The dark-haired receptionist smiled. The tips of her hair were dyed orange. Luna admired the shade similar to cup coral before she murmured, "Um, I don't have a reservation, but I spoke with Cemil—"

"Oh, that explains it." The receptionist scooped up a line of playing cards and randomly shuffled them. "Yeah, we had a cancelation just this morning, and now you're here to fill the spot. Perfect."

Relief washed over Luna at her good fortune. Plus the reasonable room rate the receptionist mentioned put her at ease.

"I'm Myron, by the way. And here is your room key. You'll find, at the Wiccan Haus, while you don't always get what you asked for, we strive to give you what you need—and so you'll find a saltwater tap in your bathtub."

"Wow, thanks." Luna gazed at the name tag on Myron's uniform. It read Trixie. Distracted by the obvious name confusion, Luna turned away with her room key—slamming into a hard wall of flesh. Sirens, in general, were on the small side. All the ones she knew were no taller than five feet; most resembled adolescents. The man she bumped into towered over her. She retreated one step, wrinkling her nose at the pungent smell—her nose had rammed the broad bones between the man's nipples. She rubbed the soreness away with her palm. He stayed rooted to his spot while she took another rearward step. Dried mud encased the man's worn boots. Dirt-smudged legs covered in dark hair disappeared into his tattered cargo shorts. At his waist, through the faded Army-green T-shirt, his muscular body expanded up and out like the trunk of a tree to his broad shoulders and shapely, hard limbs. Immediately, her thoughts conjured her water god. She had never seen anyone as tall or physically perfect as her god—until now. Perfect, despite the grime.

She arched her neck, throat stretched, and she slowly raised her gaze in curiosity. A shaggy beard hung from his face; his thick eyebrows were drawn together as he penetrated her with his gaze. The fern-green of his eyes resembled the forests beyond the Wiccan Haus. Lucky for her, smell wasn't her strongest sense because a tang filled her nostrils. Her keen eyesight assessed the tower in front of her—a scruffy, smelly mountain man—ew.

"Excuse me, miss," he said.

The deep baritone voice left its vibration under her skin. Dropping her hand from her nose, she rubbed the gooseflesh on her arm. She nodded hastily, dashing around him, and then crossed the lobby to the elevator. Pushing the elevator button, she fiddled with the room key and watched the woodsman across the room. His broad shoulders evoked images of the water god and sparked a longing within her. Oh, how she had spent hours rubbing oil into clusters of muscles, rolling like hills and valleys under her small hands.

Something near the man's shoulder caught her eye. Out of the woven dreads in his waist-long hair poked a furry face.

Gross! He has a rodent living on him! What a shame. If he wasn't so mangy....

The elevator opened, and Luna hastened into the empty chamber. She gave the woodsman a fleeting look before the doors closed. She pressed number two, and it illuminated. Number two—her second chance. She came here to heal, not make friends, and certainly not to find romance.

What was I thinking?

***

"Nathaniel Quinn is it you under all that scruff?" Myron smiled at him, lifted the deck of cards, and skillfully shuffled them in her bejeweled hands.

"I couldn't stay away."

They both knew he never came to the island for

pleasure.

"Oh, so you're here for rest and relaxation? A makeover perhaps?" The receptionist had known him a long time. She flipped over one card face up and was about to flip another, but she stopped when the door to the security office opened and the head of security stepped out. She briefly glanced over.

Nate laughed at her last comment regarding a makeover. Some of the other human passengers on the ferry gawked at his unkempt appearance. Clearing his throat, he ran his fingers through his scruffy hair. "I'm in desperate need of a haircut and a beard trimming. Can I make an appointment in the spa?"

"For you, there is an immediate opening. Let me get your room key, and you can head right in whenever you're ready." She stashed her cards and collected his key.

Taking his key, he winked a thanks to Myron. She smiled charmingly and calmly despite the head of security scrutinizing them. Nate's nostrils flared, picking up the distinct scent of his weretiger friend. Impatience rolled off the security officer Rekkus, who waited to speak to him.

His long strides ate up the room's expanse, and he stopped short of pulling Rekkus into a bear hug when he saw the man's displeased expression.

"What the fuck happened to you?" Rekkus asked under his breath.

"I was away from home with my sled dogs on business when you contacted me. I came as quickly as I could."

Rekkus tipped his head in the direction of the security office, but his expression changed when Cemil entered the lobby.

"I need a moment." Rekkus moved to head off Cemil while Nate walked into the darkened room lit by a wall of digital monitors.

One of the four owners sat behind a desk. Cyrus Rowan lifted his brows.

"Excuse my scruffiness, sir, but I came straight away," Nate said.

"We are lucky to have you, Nate. Rekkus was convinced you put the Para Elite force in your past."

"With a threat to the island and your safety, well, sir, you've done a lot for me." Nate never forgot the people who had his six. Years ago, after he had taken out an entire coven of rouge vampires, he'd been severly injured. His team got him to the Wiccan Haus, and the staff had eventually healed him.

Cyrus nodded. "So, I heard a rumor you're

breeding sled dogs in northern Canada now?"

"Yes. My associate is running affairs while I'm away." Nate bent to set his backpack on the floor against the wall and tugged at the zipper. He made a subtle sucking noise between his teeth while holding the pack open. A blur of fur scurried the length of his arm and dropped inside the safety of the worn canvas bag. He stood and faced Cyrus again.

Cyrus stared at the pack only a moment; he made no comment about what he saw.

Nate was grateful for Cyrus's reserve. He'd tried to leave the red squirrel behind. The persistent squirrel had followed him for five hundred miles before Nate gave up trying to ditch him. The little furball had stuck with him ever since the day Nate rescued him two years ago; he couldn't help the little woodland animal bonded with him.

Cemil entered the office followed by Rekkus, who closed the door, giving them privacy. Cemil was exasperated. "Don't the guests read the brochure? I was outside again apologizing to visitors that cell phones don't work on the island. And I reminded them it's clearly stated on our website. People just can't unplug."

"Yes, well, we have a more important matter to

discuss, Cemil," Cyrus said to his brother.

Rekkus crossed his arms over his solid chest and leaned against the desk Cyrus sat behind. Nate took in the vision of the two men. They were best friends, both dressed in black, and both wearing the same blank expressions with their gazes pinned on Cemil. Nate sensed Cemil's discomfort at their unforgiving stares and intense attention.

"What did I do?" Cemil's voice raised a notch, unwilling to own up to his obvious indiscretion. He turned his head and fiddled with his hair, avoiding their scrutiny. Suddenly, he noticed Nate. "Oh, hello." Cemil gave him a once over.

Nate shifted uncomfortably, gave a curt nod, and averted his attention to Rekkus.

"Who is that? She's not on the list." Rekkus pointed to a paused screen, the still-shot magnified.

Nate stared at the image of a girl—the same girl who'd bumped into him at the front desk a few minutes ago. She wore the same dress, but the picture had been captured outdoors. He surmised the footage was from earlier today. His body tensed. How had this lovely young woman caused Rekkus's disgruntlement?

Cemil seemed to reluctantly peel his gaze from Nate and followed Rekkus's finger to the screen. He raised his eyebrows. "That's Luna. She is sort of…a siren—but not from this realm. She swam onto the beach."

Cyrus said, "We know she swam onto the beach. Myron warned us someone gifted would break through the magical barrier."

Not much slipped past Myron, Nate silently accepted. It seemed her cards often forewarned of potential threats, although Nate hadn't sensed anything unusual in Myron's exchange with the siren. Apparently, the cards had their limits.

"Right. Only Myron told me first. So I took security with me to see who it could be. And there it is, I met Luna." Cemil crossed his arms over his chest.

"Cemil, why have you allowed a stranger to stay at a time when the Syndicate warns of an assassination attempt on your brother's life?" Rekkus asked and gestured toward Cyrus, who didn't move a muscle.

Nate anchored his attention on Cyrus, recalling prior threats. Cyrus Rowan had a bounty on his head. Rekkus's concern was justifiable, but Nate was conflicted with the target. He didn't see this delicate beauty as *that* kind of threat. Nate understood being head of security for the island was a monstrous responsibility, and, to add to his pressure, Rekkus was also Cyrus's personal bodyguard. For this trip, Nate's sole assignment was to flush out threats. He would answer to these men.

"Poor, little thing has had her heart broken. I knew it the moment I touched her hand. I believe she is only here to heal, Rekkus," Cemil said.

Cemil's gift as an empath gave him a true sense of people when he touched them. His opinion of Luna filled Nate with relief. Nate glimpsed at the monitor, committing her profile to memory.

"I don't like coincidences. A para cancels last minute, and then this siren conveniently slips past our underwater details and waltzes in here. We know nothing about her. She could be dangerous." Rekkus scowled at Cemil.

Nate hid a grin when Cemil flung his hands up and shook them with mock fear. He bit his lip when Cemil waved dismissively and said, "Oh, Rekkus, all sirens are *dangerous*."

The weretiger growled.

Rekkus took security very seriously—in fact, he took everything seriously. Contained rage oozed from the man at Cemil's careless teasing.

"However"—Cemil said after his brother narrowed his eyes at him—"I don't sense she's here to harm anyone. Cyrus has nothing to fear from that little guppy. Also, I informed her she'd need to sign a contract regarding her *songs*."

Cyrus tapped his leather-covered finger on the desk. "I have an idea." The three men turned their attention to Cyrus, who leaned forward, placing his gloved hands together. "While Nate is here undercover, we can have him watch her...befriend her...find out why she's really here. Maybe she knows something?"

Cemil gazed over his shoulder at Nate. "I thought you looked familiar. I didn't recognize you with all that...hair." He smiled, amusement glinting in his eyes. "Are you trying to connect with your inner-species?"

Nate grinned and let the teasing slide. His species, the Sasquatch who roamed northern Canada, were sought after by the Syndicate's Elite force because of their sheer size and strength. Problem was most were loners, and many had gentler sides not conducive for combat. Nate knew these plights all too well; however, the Syndicate paid generously.

Ignoring Cemil's snickering, Nate focused on the image of the siren. From the moment he'd stepped into the lobby earlier, he'd picked up her scent. Steadily, he'd followed it until he stood close behind her. Like a deer drawn to a saltlick, his urge to touch her...taste her lips...had been overwhelming. He'd been so close, when she swung around, her long, black hair brushed his clothes. For the first time in his life, he froze while his brain ran diagnostics on his body. What had he felt? It was the true and urgent pull of wild instinct and heightened senses onset by this girl. Trying to recover from his shock and confusion, he'd gulped and forced his breathing to remain steady. When she'd abruptly bumped her nose to his chest, he prayed he acted normal instead of appearing like a starved bear sniffing honey. The accidental touch had sent a jolt through him. But nothing compared to when she'd tilted her head and blasted him with her eyes, as clear and large as a starless winter night. Then, to his greatest disappointment, she had wrinkled her nose, dismissed him, and moved away. Maybe she hadn't recognized it—but he had. He had just found his mate.

"That's an interesting idea." Nate cleared his throat, wondering how this could happen. The potential threat was his destined mate.

Rekkus straightened to his full 6'5" frame and crossed to the totem pole of a man. "Could work." He nodded. "Luna is your new detail."

A weary chuckle escaped Nate at his sticky

predicament as he absorbed the weight of his assignment.

The weretiger scrunched his nose. "You're not going to entice anyone with your rank earthiness. Get cleaned up, and we'll have a briefing this evening after the meal is served. You must attend like the rest of the guests since you're undercover."

Cemil seemed to breathe through his mouth and griped, "He's not wrong. Though the smell of *man* is tempting, your smell is a bit overwhelming. Not to mention your clothes are in bad need of washing...or burning."

Nate's attention snapped to Rekkus. *Did the weretiger just laugh?*

Chapter Two

The mandatory dinner hour forced Luna to leave the comfort of her room. The smell of cooked meat hit her nose as soon as the elevator door opened. She diverted to the front desk to drop off the signed "no singing or humming" contract delivered to her room earlier. Myron accepted it with a reassuring smile.

Again, the aroma of cooked foods wafted past her. Reluctantly following the scent, she slowed her pace as she passed the lodge's boutique and sundries shop. The colorful sundresses and accessories displayed in its wide, glass windows caused her to run her hand over her clothing. She'd swum to the island in the one dress she wore now. Excessive clothing in the ocean was impractical, so it had slipped her mind to pack any extra. But now she was among others—out of the water—the dresses, as colorful as coral, intrigued her. Luna couldn't wait to try them on but couldn't do so now because the boutique was closed during dining hours. She cursed under her breath.

In the reflection of the window, two blonde women passed behind her, commenting loudly on the bikinis also appealingly displayed. Luna waited for the blondes to disappear through the open doors at the end of the hallway before she followed them.

Entering the room, she was disappointed every table already had guests, though there were a few empty seats among them. The two blondes had taken the last vacant table. Something about their giggly, bubbly demeanors annoyed Luna, and so there was no way she was sitting with them. Determined to find somewhere else to sit, she spotted a lone man at the corner table with a book in his hand. Older and distinguished, he appeared harmless enough, so she advanced in his direction. Dread churned in her stomach at the thought of eating with these humans.

Maybe coming here wasn't such a good idea.

Just as the man set his book aside and a polite smile spread across his face, Luna noticed a second room with more seating. Without giving the man another thought, she veered right and crossed into the other space. A strange feeling passed over her. Scanning the room, she concluded no humans dined in there. She scurried to the closest empty table and sat down with relief. However, just inside the main dining room adjacent to her table and in her direct line of sight sat the blondes. *Er.*

One blonde flirted with their waiter, and her husky voice grated on Luna's nerves. Glancing around the backroom, she found the guests in here a bit more...exotic. Though she sensed they were nonhuman, she couldn't exactly detect what they were.

"Look at that tall, dark, and doable man," the blonde with the husky voice said.

Interest piqued, Luna leaned slightly forward to get a better angle on the entrance. An exceptionally tall and broad man strode in, his manner casual and easy. He paused when Cemil stopped to speak with him. Brows drawing together, she scrutinized him. *It can't be.* But how many men could possibly be as big as the one she'd bumped into at check-in? He wasn't the same—exactly. This man had thick, wavy brown hair to his shoulders, and his dark beard was trim and stylish around his strong jawline. His white linen shirt was crisp, and his navy shorts were pressed with creases. He was a larger model of the Nantucket yachters she'd seen off the Massachusetts coast.

Wow. What a transformation! She couldn't stop staring.

"I'd like to lock my legs around him," the other blonde commented to her friend.

"I wonder if he's big everywhere?" The husky pitch

rose higher. They both preened and tittered.

Sinfully, Luna wondered the same thing. A strange flutter started in her belly then melted south. She squirmed in her seat. Snatching the menu, she held it up in front of her face, but her gaze lingered on the woodsman above the laminated paper. Cemil glanced in her direction, as did the woodsman. Luna shrunk behind the menu. After a few seconds, she peeked over the top again only to panic when he walked her way.

"Ooh Lord, he's coming this way," one blonde said.

They tossed their hair and beamed smiles at him as he approached, but he passed them by.

Luna set her menu down and scanned the tables, wondering who the sexy stranger would sit with. He'd fit right in with the shaggy wolf shifters who ate and laughed boisterously across the room. At least, she was fairly certain they were wolf shifters. The stranger reached her table in only a few long strides.

"Good evening. May I join you?"

The fresh scent of pine wafted off him, and she inhaled deeper, contemplating an excuse. Surprisingly, she couldn't think of one. She breathed out a pent-up exhale. Obliged, she offered the free chair. Instead of staring at him, she stole a look at the blondes who slouched with disappointed pouts on their mouths. Their sullen letdown shouldn't have meant anything to Luna—but it did.

"I'm Nathaniel Quinn—Nate." He held his hand out.

She stared at his paw of a hand for a moment before she slipped hers into his. It was warm, and the palm was calloused.

"Luna, just Luna." She withdrew her hand and dropped it to her lap where she smoothed the short skirt of her dress.

"What brings you to the Wiccan Haus?"

"I'm here for relaxation and rejuvenation," she said. "And you?"

"The same. I came south for the warmer weather."

"Oh." She scanned the room for the waiter. If she could just get her dinner, she could eat quickly and leave. This giant's presence overwhelmed her, and, when he smiled at her...she somehow forgot to breathe.

"Yeah, I came down from Canada. I raise sled dogs. Some run races like the Iditarod. I do hate leaving them, though."

She'd never heard of dog races or the Iditarod. But hearing about the animals made her recall seeing a furry face nestled in among this woodsman's clothing earlier. "What happened to your stowaway?"

When recognition reached his eyes, they twinkled with mirth. She tingled at the deep vibrations of his laughter.

"You must mean the cheeky fellow about this big." He stretched his thumb and pointer finger to indicate the size of his beady-eyed friend.

"What is it?"

"He's a red squirrel. He fell from a tree when he was a baby, and I nursed him back to health. The little guy stuck around." He lifted one bulky shoulder. The shirt fabric strained against it.

"What do you call him?"

Elbows on the table, he held up a palm and shook his head. "I didn't name him."

"He sounds like a pet."

"He's not."

She prodded. "Do you name the dogs?"

"Well, yeah, but the sled dogs are for my business." It seemed he failed to see the connection.

The waiter stopped at Nate's elbow. "Have you decided?"

Luna picked hers up and scouting for the sushi Cemil promised. Thankfully, it was first on the list, and she pointed to the item she wanted.

"We also have ahi tuna with an Asian glaze for tonight's special."

"Sounds perfect. It's my favorite." Nate handed over the menu.

While the waiter jotted down their meals and drink orders, Luna made a mental note that Nate loved ahi tuna...*and* he ordered it rare. Surprised, she'd expected him to order a plate of red meat. How coincidental they were both being served their favorite meals at the Wiccan Haus.

Should she start a conversation? She fiddled with her napkin for a moment, not sure what to say next. If she didn't, he might catch on to how much his nearness rattled her. Then he laughed again, and his warm, good-humored personality put her at ease. Soon, she was smiling at his amusing sled dog stories. The waiter returned and delivered their drinks. Luna gratefully took several generous sips of wine, guessing the heat in her cheeks had to be from the alcohol because she wasn't one to blush—ever. She might resemble a teenager, but she was over two hundred years old.

Dinner arrived, and she didn't rush to eat but, instead, savored the food while listening to his stories.

To her delight, Cemil was right about how fresh the sushi was. With her stomach content, she leaned into her chair and watched the waiter remove their plates.

Nate set down his drink. "So, tell me more about you. Where are you from?" He smiled at her.

She returned his smile much less enthusiastically. What could she say? "I'm from nowhere in particular. I move around a lot."

"Do you move around for your job? What do you do?"

"Do? Um. I make therapies for the skin like soaps and oils. And I make herb and spice combinations to enhance the seafood I prepare." It wasn't a lie. She did it for the water god. Several guests had finished their meals and left the dining room. Before Nate could say anything else, she swiftly slid out her chair and stood. "It was nice talking to you."

He viewed her with surprise. "Yes, I enjoyed talking with you as well. I'm sure we'll see each other again—and I look forward to it."

She lifted a slender shoulder, agreeing it could be a possibility, but she couldn't help grinning and hoping it was. "Good night, Nate." Walking away, her nostrils flared again, inhaling his earthy scent.

"Good night, Luna."

What was it about Nathaniel Quinn? Why did he linger in her thoughts? Up until her arrival on the island, she was consumed with how and why she hadn't been enough for the water god. She realized now, if she hadn't come to the Wiccan Haus, her obsession would have driven her to madness. She'd never forget the bitter sting of betrayal, but the sting had dulled since meeting Nate.

His strikingly handsome image was lodged in her cerebrum. She'd had to force herself to look elsewhere or be caught staring at his hair; its textured darkness was like bark after a rainstorm. It beckoned to her, tempting her to reach out and touch it. Lost in thought and imagining her hands in his hair, before she knew it, she walked past the boutique. She skated to a stop and grinned. The shop was open. Thoughts of Nate evaporated as the tailored merchandise filled her vision.

An hour later, Luna arrived at her door, holding a generously bulging shopping bag with the Wiccan Haus logo on it. She had been alone in the elevator, yet a sudden breeze tugged the tendrils of hair around her temples. When she turned in its direction, a man she'd seen downstairs stood next to her. He'd sat at a table in the same room. The only reason she remembered him was because he, and the guests at his table, only ordered drinks—tall glasses of red liquid. She regretted giving him a polite smile earlier when their gazes met across the dining room, though he was handsome in a dark and mysterious way.

"Hello, beautiful, why don't you invite me in?" He casually leaned against the doorjamb and lifted his manicured brows.

How did he sneak up on me? The stories she'd heard of blood-drinking beings came to mind. *He must be a vampire.*

"I'm not in the habit of inviting strange men into my room." Annoyed by his arrogance, she glared at him.

He ignored her remark and went on as if she hadn't spoken. "You know, I bet you have an amazing voice."

"What?" Panic made her voice go hoarse. Apparently, her kind was easily detected by nonhumans. On this side of the realm, this would be a weary adjustment, especially when she was new to encountering a variety of nonhumans.

He smiled—a mouth open, teeth-showing grin.

Fangs! Yes, definitely a vampire. She grumbled under her breath.

"Don't let the fangs scare you, little siren. You could sing to me all night, and it would have no effect. You could sing...scream...sing. Whatever while we—"

"Oh, is that right?" she asked, her composure regained, never one to fear others.

He thinks my singing is my only weapon. Ha! Her singing and underwater lifestyle labeled her a siren, but her species had a little something extra.

"What about *my* teeth?" Her innocent looks gave people a sense she was delicate and defenseless—the allure was part of her charm. Luna found it gratifying to let her inner monster show, like now, when she was pissed off. With a jerk to her neck, she unhinged her jaw allowing her mouth to open unusually wide as her lips parted like a freak show clown. The soft flesh of her cheeks gathered at her ears while her razor-sharp secondary teeth slid from her gums and jutted in his direction. The vampire recoiled. She only stayed transformed for a moment—just enough to see the vampire's smug grin slip away like a receding wave.

"Impressive. A shark in a mermaid's body." He stood straighter, trying to look suave after his apparent shock.

"I'm not a mermaid. I don't have a tail. I'm a siren from another realm. Learn the difference, you ignorant bat."

"Your words are as sharp as your teeth. Good evening, siren."

A swoosh of air was all that remained of his presence. Luna breathed a sigh of relief.

Chapter Three

After a restful sleep, Luna woke to the cries of seagulls. Their pitchy screeches made her thankful flying birds never evolved in her realm. Her stomach grumbled, driving her from the soft bed and into the bathroom. She smiled at the tub she soaked in last night, crediting it with her peaceful slumber. The basin contained traces of dry salt.

Freshened up, she reentered the bedroom and found a note slipped under her door. She swooped down to retrieve it. The invitation was from Selena for a private hydrotherapy session. The note stated she was to meet Selena by the lake this morning at ten. Glancing at the clock, Luna still had an hour before her session.

Clad in the swimsuit she purchased last night in the boutique, she grabbed the matching wrap and adjusted it around her slender waist. The ensemble was one of many newly purchased outfits and accessories. She slipped her feet into a pair of confining sandals and wiggled her toes. The excitement over her new footwear waned as she paraded around her room getting a feel for them. Determined to wear her fashionable sandals, she snatched her satchel and left the room.

Luna exited the elevator and drifted toward the breakfast bar. She wrinkled her nose at the smell of coffee. Guests grazed the offerings. About to turn away, she glimpsed a tray of smoked salmon on a cracker. Filling a plate, she sat in a quiet corner to eat and hoped to be left alone. She stood as soon as the last bite touched her lips, leaving behind a plate of stripped crackers.

Outside, the salty air rejuvenated her almost instantly, lifting her spirits higher. Could she hope for a new beginning? She followed a floral-lined path, unexpectedly appreciative of the nature around her. A tiny, yellow bird flittered from tree to tree. Its birdsong was substantially different than the seagull's cry, and, surprisingly, it enchanted her. When the bird bounded farther into the trees, away from the path, Luna felt compelled to follow it. The pine trees grew closer together while more and more colorful birds appeared in them, singing in concert. She wandered farther into the woods. Male voices echoed in the distance disturbing her serenity.

In a far-off clearing beyond the thick brush, three

men stood, talking. Two of them wore all black. The third was Nathaniel Quinn. She froze; her shoulders tensed. Why seeing Nate rattled her more than the others, she didn't know. All she knew was she didn't belong here in the woods, off the beaten path, where it could be interpreted she was spying on them. Her light feet carried her away in near silence. However, not five hundred yards away, she encountered another man. He peered through slim binoculars in the direction she was trying to avoid. She thought she might slip past him unseen, but he lowered the binoculars a moment too soon.

"Oh, hey there!" He spoke just loud enough for her ears.

Meeting a stranger in the woods put her on alert. She eyed his wood-carved walking stick, his pocketed vest, and his ball cap with an embroidered bird. She blinked her large eyes at him. *Hmm, I almost sat with him in the dining room last night.*

"Are you a fellow birder, by chance?" He adjusted his cap and tapped at the lettering.

"Er, I was just taking a walk." She continued to move in the direction of the path, leaving him to his pursuit.

However, he followed her. He progressed quickly

for a man with a cane and caught up to her.

She kept a steady pace, unable to shake her uneasiness.

"Did you see anyone else out here?" he asked casually.

She swiveled to look at him, thinking it an odd question. It seemed like his binoculars were trained on the three men—not the feathered animals.

Her questioning expression seemed to get him talking. He stammered, "Well, you see, it's the birds. They seemed to have been startled by someone or something. Perhaps you startled them."

The trees opened to a clearing of grass sprawling toward the path. Luna sighed, thankful to escape.

"Where are my manners? My name is Charlie. Birdwatching is a hobby of mine, and my doctor gave me orders to rest my knee after a bad fall. So, I came to Wiccan Haus to kill two birds with one stone as they say...two birds...one stone. Because I like birds." His goofy grin revealed crooked teeth. "Sorry I get nervous around pretty girls." He hid momentarily under the brim of his cap.

The water god often vowed I was the most beautiful of all the sirens and my voice held no comparison. Her stomach rolled at Charlie's last comment. *Flattery from this walrus. Ukk.*

Before she could fire off a snarky remark, a yellow bird swooped past, catching her attention. It landed on a bench situated at the path's edge. She halted, realizing it was the same species she'd followed into the woods. Charlie stumbled to a stop as well and seemed pleasantly surprised. He ginned at her expectantly.

Deciding to give the poor fellow a break from her serpent's tongue, Luna pointed. "Look. The yellow one is beautiful. What's it called?"

"Oh, indeed!" Charlie raised his sleek mini binoculars though the animal wasn't far away. "Mmhmm. Indeed. Very rare. I'll have to consult my guidebook." He set the binoculars against his lean chest and tugged a camera from a vest pocket.

Luna reluctantly stood still until he took the snapshot. She prepared to bolt—it was time to lose this guy.

A sudden, loud rustling behind them sent the delicate creature into flight. A deep, authoritative voice bellowed, "I'll take that camera."

Luna and Charlie spun around. Two men dressed in black stood outlined by the pines.

"Oh. Oh, dear. Who are you?" Charlie shuffled

about, gripping the knob of his cane.

"Rekkus, head of security." Rekkus tipped his head in the other man's direction. "Cyrus Rowan."

Rowan. The four Rowan siblings run the Wiccan Haus. Luna eyed Cemil's brother but found the head of security more interesting. *What are you, Rekkus?*

Rekkus prowled over. Charlie rapidly pushed several buttons and turned off the camera. Luna's thoughts quickly shifted to Nate. Why had the three men met in seclusion? And where had Nate gone?

"I was simply shooting wildlife, sir," Charlie said.

"Cameras are not permitted on the island. We strive to preserve the privacy of our guests. I will have your property returned to you upon your departure." Rekkus held out his hand.

Luna took this distraction to speak up. "I have an appointment. I don't want to be late, so I'll see you at dinner."

Cyrus gave her a pleasant nod. The other two barely gave her a glance as they discussed the confiscation of Charlie's equipment. Scanning the trees for Nate one last time, something shimmery caught her eye. The translucent shape appeared in man-like form. Fascinated, but not wanting to miss her opportunity to slip away, she continued toward the path without a backward glance.

Luna met the path's end, a smile on her lips. The saltwater lake beckoned her, though she hesitated when she noticed the instructor talking to another woman, likely the appointment before hers concluding. After the two women finished talking and the guest strolled away, Luna approached the hydrotherapy instructor.

"Hello, you must be Luna. I'm Selena."

Luna closed the gap between them and shook the hand Selena offered. "It's nice to meet you, Selena."

Their gazes locked, an immediate connection registered for both of them.

"Wow, you're really her—*the* Selena from the royal mermaid family," Luna said a little breathy.

Selena smoothed her pale hair from the crown of her head down to the tightly woven braid hanging over her slender shoulder.

"So, you've heard of me?" She seemed flattered.

Luna glanced around to ensure their privacy. "Yes, you...and your kind. The sisterhood where I'm from told me stories about your family and how you left them."

"Yes, Luna, I've managed to break tradition. You can, too. I already see it in you—strength and bravery.

I will help you. You shouldn't fear change."

What did Cemil tell you?

"I'm not like you. You wouldn't understand." Luna was quick to dismiss Selena's advice.

Selena assured, "Siren...Mermaid, we are not so different."

She had a point. They were similar species. However, Luna wasn't ready to become fast friends just yet. She tested the waters first and pointed out their biggest difference. "You have a tail."

While Selena stood on her shapely legs out of the water, she indeed could transform in only a shallow depth. "A fin," Selena corrected. A smile tugged at the corners of her mouth.

Okay, she doesn't rile easily.

At the mention of a fin, Luna's curiosity piqued. "I have never seen your kind, though I've swum in these oceans numerous times."

"We stay hidden."

Luna understood this. Sirens revealed themselves only when they wanted to be seen. "We don't hide. We don't fear the people where I come from. The clans and tribes fear us."

"Mmhmm." Selena's expression softened in understanding.

After hesitating and scanning the tree line again, Luna returned her gaze to her instructor. "Selena, can I ask you something?"

"Of course, I'm here to help you. I will be open and honest. You can talk to me about anything."

"Do your sisters drown their lovers, too?" Luna detested the act—detested she couldn't control her bloodlust.

"I'm afraid it is a practice among our kind." Selena nodded and wrinkled her nose.

Luna swallowed the lump in her throat. She'd finally met someone who understood both the impact and implications of such crimes and, most importantly, agreed with her. For the first time, she'd found someone outside of her sisterhood who cared about what they did. The sirens at home lacked compassion—but they hadn't been loved and cherished by a god. The water god changed Luna more than just physically.

Despite their pasts, Luna sensed Selena's current contentment. "How do you deal with it, knowing your options for love and companionship are limited?"

Selena's lovely eyes sparkled. "I made a change and came here to the Wiccan Haus. It's truly splendid I fell in love. I'm now married, and no longer have that burden. And being away from my aquatic family has allowed me to live a better suited life."

"You're married!" How had this juicy detail not made it into her realm?

Selena flashed a brilliant smile and sent her a wink. "Yes, *and* my husband is human."

Luna hadn't considered a siren loving a human enough to marry him. Yet this mermaid, so like herself, had done it. She was the picture of contentment. *Could I find contentment, love, and a purpose?*

"It seems this human has made you very happy." Doubt and jealousy fueled her words.

"Oh, Luna, your heartache is temporary. The one you yearn for was not meant to be. You will understand when you love again. You will know the right man when he looks at you like you are the most important, precious treasure on earth. I have no doubt you will love again, but you must be open to it. Unlock your heart."

Luna considered her sage advice. Her desire to challenge this woman left her; somehow, Selena inspired her. She could almost be a friend—if Luna could have true friendship. The sirens she associated with at home were coldhearted and would turn on each other over a minnow.

"Shall we go for a swim?" Selena suggested. The tone of her voice lightened when she added, "A word of warning...you may get *tail envy*, siren." The mermaid's eyes sparkled with teasing mischief.

Luna lightheartedly retorted, "Not likely. I'll never be mistaken for a fish."

Selena mocked an insulted scowl followed by her dazzling smile, and the two entered the clear and calm lake. No one would ever mistake the fair and gorgeous Selena for a fish.

***

Nate spent the last couple hours on surveillance after leaving Rekkus and Cemil in the security office. The camera Rekkus confiscated from the birdwatching guest was empty save a few shots of the ferry and a yellow bird. With Luna occupied at a hydrotherapy session, he trailed and struck up conversations with guests, all the while assessing their true intent there. Though Luna had shown up unannounced at a time when the threat against Cyrus Rowan was imminent, he wasn't convinced she was the prime suspect. If any harm came to Cyrus Rowan by her hand—or voice—he couldn't imagine what he'd do. His only instinct right now was to protect her...and to make love to her.

Nate strode down the path leading to the lake and sat on the bench where he'd last seen her, waiting for her return to the Haus. He drummed his fingers on his thigh and hummed a tune in his head. After five minutes, he stood and faced the tree line. Hours ago, he'd watched Rekkus and Cyrus confront Luna and the other guest. He'd remained hidden there—cloaked and invisible—yet she had looked right at him before she walked away.

Could she see me? No. Impossible.

He glanced down the empty path again. The sun was high overhead, and he was warm from his pacing. *She should have returned by now.* Finally, female voices floated from the direction he'd been surveilling. Luna and Selena rounded the bend.

"Hey, Nate," Luna said when the girls reached him.

"Hi, ladies." He didn't want Luna to know he'd been waiting for her. He crossed his arms and tried not to appear awkward standing around. Selena's widened eyes confirmed his fears. The staff members, who knew Nate, had been informed he was undercover, posing as a guest.

Selena said to Luna, "If you'll excuse me, I have another appointment in the spa. Enjoy your yoga class." Selena glanced at the sun, and said to Luna. "It should be starting very soon."

"Oh, are you taking the noon yoga class, too?" he asked Luna.

"Yes, but I think it's held on the lawn behind the Haus." Luna seemed puzzled as to why he was heading in the opposite direction.

"Right. I was thinking it was down by the lake." He flashed a smile in Selena's direction before turning to Luna. "Good thing I ran into you."

"I'll see you tomorrow, Luna."

Selena and Luna exchanged a wave, and Selena moved gracefully down the path.

"Do you mind if I walk with you?" Nate stroked his beard absentmindedly.

Luna dropped her gaze, shook her head, and quickened her pace. He fell into step beside her.

Nate struggled to engage her in casual conversation because she seemed resolved to stay standoffish. Her rigidity conveyed she felt uncomfortable around him, like she fought the attraction. He'd had her talking at dinner last night, but it took effort on his part. The path opened to a lawn bordered by green shrubs and flowers. Several guests had claimed the brightly colored mats placed in neat rows in the lush grass.

"Welcome to our deep-breathing yoga class. Please find a mat and take a seat," said a tall, ethereal woman with silver hair. "My name is Trixie, and I will be your instructor this afternoon."

Nate had befriended Trixie from his previous extended stay. She'd proved a good companion while helping him recover. Because Trixie was half fae, he connected with her in some ways. They both valued the earth, the forests, and its creatures big and small.

Trixie coached the class. "Everyone, please sit pretzel style and adjust your sit-bones. Close your eyes and take in the surroundings—the heat of the sun, the cool breeze, the sound of the waves."

Nate kept his gaze lowered and trained on Luna who sat next to him, following instructions. After lengthy inhales and exhales, too many in Nate's opinion, it was time to reposition.

"If you're ready to move on from belly breathing and meditation, then I invite you to move onto your hands and knees for some cat and cow stretches."

He remained seated while Luna shifted to all fours. Mesmerized and turned on by the way her lithe body moved, he dragged in breaths and exhaled with loud blows. Eventually, he participated, learning the positions and movements of a sun salutation. Completely out of sequence with the class, rolling like the undulating surf, he half-listened and vaguely applied himself. As Luna swept through sun salutations, his idea of meditation was staring at her perfectly shaped ass pointed in the air when she held downward dog. Oh the things he imagined doing to her in this yoga pose. Yoga was leaving his one particular muscle stiff.

"Ah, nicely done, folks. Now we will pair up for a stretching exercise." Trixie walked through the group of eight participants and paired off couples as she skipped by on nimble feet. "You two partner up." She pointed to Nate and Luna, the last couple in the row on the corner of the grass.

Nate smirked at Luna's frown. He couldn't deny she'd caught him staring at her more than once. And, oh, if he was going to be touching her, then he wished the rest of the class would spontaneously disappear. He volunteered to go first. It was important he moved about and adjusted how his cock tented in his loose-fitting shorts. He had to give himself a mental shake and shut down the compass in his pants that pointed at Luna—his new north.

Finally, mimicking the others, he lay flat, face up, arms out to a T. His gaze stayed on Luna who stood off to the side fiddling with the strap to her bikini top.

Visiting and helping each couple, Trixie reached Nate and Luna last. Trixie said to Nate, "That's a good start. Now, lift one knee and rotate it across your body. Yes, you've got it." She motioned to Luna. "Kneel here and place one hand on the side of his knee while you place the other on his shoulder." Trixie whispered in Luna's ear, "Don't be afraid to lean in. Nate is larger than most, so he could do with more pressure."

Luna slid her palms around for ideal placement. His muscles tensed. She must have felt it because her gaze flew to his.

Trixie withdrew, though her tranquil voice floated over the guests. "Gentle pressure, folks. And those laying against the earth, feel it's gravity, and breathe into the stretch."

Luna flicked her gaze to the grass. He studied her delicate profile and pink cheeks. Because of their vast size difference, Luna practically laid across his muscled torso. Her thin but shapely arms were spread as far as they could go. Her dark hair hung heavy on his chest. He wished his T-shirt would vanish so the silky strands caressed his skin. After a few moments, they had to alternate sides. And then change positions. It was her turn to lie down.

All the pairs switched places. As Luna adjusted her shoulders against the mat her black-as-ink hair fanned and trailed into the grass, and her chest rose and fell at a rapid rate. She gazed at him through rounded eyes filled with trepidation.

Do you anticipate my touch?

He anticipated touching her! With a dry swallow, he spread a huge palm across her shoulder—the base of it rested against the top of her breast while his thumb stroked her collarbone. He swore he felt her slightly arch. It took nearly all his control not to slide his hand lower and cup the firm mound of flesh. The tight peaks couldn't be hidden under the thin fabric of her bikini. When he looked into her enormous eyes, they were the darkest shade of blue he'd ever seen. His pulse sped up, and he tore his gaze away from her beautiful face. How could one tiny woman force him to come unhinged? He narrowed his focus to task. Luna caught her breath when he cupped her hip and slid his heated palm down her curvaceous thigh to clutch her knee.

He leaned down to whisper near her ear. "Is this

enough pressure? Would you like more?"

She snapped her eyes closed and shook her head. "No, it's fine."

He chuckled. This wasn't relaxing by a long shot. They were both tense and hot for each other—this exercise magnified it. After switching directions, he had to release her physically, but he was emotionally tethered to her. The class wound down with more meditation, each returned to their own mat. When the class ended, Luna hopped up and seemed ready to dash away, but she stopped and looked down, searching around her feet.

A blur of fur and an indignant squeak made her jump sideways.

Nate was at her side in a second. "Are you okay?"

She tilted her face to him, her delicate brows askew with annoyance. "I think your pet ran off with my anklet charm."

"Your what?"

"I bought an ankle bracelet in the boutique last night, and it seems the charm has fallen off." She turned her ankle out so he could see the slim gold chain around it. "It was there when we started the class."

"Oh, I see. Yeah, he's not my pet." He waved a

hand at the moot point. "Anyway, he could have taken it. He's used to me giving him odd things, though mostly food."

"Well, I want it returned. It's the first one I ever bought for myself."

Immediately, he felt responsible, and upsetting his mate wouldn't do. "No problem. We'll get it from him."

A rustling in the brush caught Nate's attention, and he strode toward the swaying perennials. He waved Luna over as he neared the flowerbed. He rolled his lips, and, with his tongue to his teeth, he made a rapid clicking sound. The squirrel lifted its head above the blooms with something metallic in its mouth. The animal trained its beady eyes on Nate.

"Come on, give it back."

Luna judged the russet, black-eyed creature. "Are you sure that thing is tame?"

Nate and Luna were the last of the guests on the lawn when Trixie strolled over.

"What's the little fellow got in its mouth?" she asked.

"My charm." Luna sighed.

"I might have just the thing for a trade." Trixie dug into her pocket and pulled out an almond. She held it up for Nate's inspection then handed it to him.

The ladies watched as Nate succeeded in a game of cat and mouse with the squirrel. The trio traipsed closer and closer to the trees, in pursuit. When a yellow bird fluttered by, Luna asked about it.

"He's an American goldfinch. They are common on the island...all over New England, too," Trixie said.

Nate made a grab for the fur ball while the girls were talking, but the red squirrel managed to scamper up into a tree before he could catch him.

He stroked his knuckles along his beard under his chin, attempting to ease his aggravation. He pondered his next move.

"Thank you, Trixie, for the class." Luna smiled.

"You're welcome, dear." Trixie called to Nate before turning in the direction of the Haus, "Good luck."

Nate stretched his palm in her direction. "Thanks for the class and the almond."

He turned his palm and motioned Luna closer. She followed him toward a squat, low-branched tree. Luna ducked under the branches and tilted her head to get a better look where Nate was pointing.

"Here, watch this." Snatching her by her waist, he effortlessly lifted her. He set her bottom on a sturdy tree branch, her face level with his. The inviting site of her parted lips held his attention. Tearing his gaze away from the tempting distraction, he held up the almond before placing it on the branch just above his head. He glanced at Luna, confident. She inspected him with interest. The red squirrel poked its head out of hiding to have a sniff. It hopped over to the nut. It dropped the charm from its mouth and picked up the almond. Nate caught the falling charm in midair, chuckling. He faced Luna with a triumphant smile.

"Yay, I could kiss you!" she exclaimed, but a rush of nervous air followed.

Her softened expression drew him to her, and he leaned toward her. "I'll take that reward," he said huskily, resting his palm on the branch by her thigh. Under the canopy of branches, it offered them a sense of privacy. Now was the perfect time to kiss her.

"Nate, I should go—"

"Luna," he said, low and urgent. He abandoned the textured tree bark to caress the tips of her fingers, sliding his hand up the soft slope of her arm. "Don't you feel what is between us?"

She peeked at him through her long and lush lashes. "I find you...very...um, *extremely* attractive, but I don't think we should pursue this...whatever *this* is."

"I don't think we can deny it." Creeping his lips

closer to hers, he paused. She didn't flinch, just stared into his eyes.

The pull proved strong and unyielding.

Encouraged, he leaned farther and captured her lips. She responded to his slow assault by parting her lips, allowing his inevitable invasion. He gripped her to him, hard and forceful, as he touched his tongue to hers, swirling and caressing. Her deep moan excited him, and he thrust his tongue deeper, seemingly driving her wild. She clutched his shoulders, giving him more of her talented kisses, sucking and nibbling on his lips. The wildly erotic feel of her sent his cock stretching toward her, hot and diamond hard. When her thighs clamped around his waist, he reached down, squeezing her tight, little ass. A low growl escaped his throat as he cupped her flesh and jerked her against his hard point. He arched and flexed his pelvis against her. The tip of his cock stretched beyond the waistband of his shorts and a bead of cum left a sticky line on her flat, bare abdomen. Primed for penetration and sweet release, he murmured her name between kisses.

A screech from above momentarily broke his kissing, but, after a scarce glance, he resumed with fervor. His heart pumped, and his cock throbbed. His call to mate with her was the strongest sensation he'd ever felt. He needed to stop before he took her here and now against the tree.

He lifted her slightly to reseat her on the branch before releasing her exquisitely formed bottom. Her legs slid off him, and her grip spanned his shoulders. Though he had to force his hands off her delicious behind, he still had to touch her. Stroking her curved hip with one hand, he steadied himself with the other by gripping the branch.

You are more than I could have imagined or hoped for in a passionate mate—and all we did was kiss. I can't fathom what it will be like to feel myself inside you. He shuddered at the thought.

He slowed his invasion of her mouth and pulled away just enough to brand kisses across her flushed cheek and around her earlobe. When she sighed, he smiled against the warm, salty skin of her neck. He lifted his head and waited for her to open her eyes. When she did—wow—dilated and filled with hunger for him. His mate wanted him as much as he wanted her. Oh how he wanted this issue with Cyrus resolved. He wanted Luna cleared of suspicion so he could lay claim to her.

"Luna, why did you come here...to the Wiccan Haus?"

"I told you—"

"Tell me the truth. Tell me everything." There was more to it, he just knew. He only hoped it had nothing to do with Cyrus Rowan.

She leaned her head to the side, her expression confused at first. She removed her hands from his torso; scorn replaced the passion in her eyes. "I was with…I was in a relationship. At least, I thought I was part of the relationship. It turned out I wasn't *the one* for him. But I realize now… I never was. I was so blinded by the gifts he gave me…." Her eyes slowly blinked like she was changing the pictures viewed in her mind. "I won't be used again. Nate, for your sake, it's best if I'm alone."

His inner monster raged at the depth of her pain. "You must know I can never leave you alone. Not after I've found my mate."

"Mate!" She wiggled her rump, forcing him to step back so she could jump down. "Pick another mate!"

"It doesn't work that way. I don't pick. It—fate—it picks me. It is the way of my kind."

"I don't know your kind. Who, or what, are you, Nate?"

Yes, he needed to explain to her about his species—at a later time. "But you must feel it. Tell me you feel it!" *Damn! I don't like what's happening to me. I'm reduced to pleading.* "This is just as unexpected for me as it is for you."

She shook her head. "No. And you don't know *my* kind. You don't know what we do to those we desire. Please, Nate, just let it go. Forget about me."

He placed his hand on her arm, but she shoved past him. The turmoil he felt was foreign. He let her go, agony burning in his gut. When he hung his head in defeat, he noticed the little charm nestled in the grass. He bent to retrieve it. Holding it in his palm, he chuckled. It was a heart—he held her heart.

Chapter Four

Luna dried her hair with a hair dryer for the first time. She stood in front of the bathroom mirror, tossing her head this way and that, admiring the smooth, glossy, black waves. Satisfied, she moved on to her lips, adding a smear of pink gloss. The tube advertised cherries, and the wand smelled like the fruit. She swiped her tongue across her lip for a taste. *Mmm, tasty.* She wondered if Nate would like the taste of cherries on her lips—if he kissed her again.

"Not going to happen," she said to her reflection.

She set her recent purchase on the sink counter and left the bathroom. The evening sunset cast her room in an orange glow, and she glanced longingly out the window at the sparkling water. With a heavy sigh, she found her sandals by the door where she'd kicked them off last night. The offenders had left little blisters on her heels, and she couldn't imagine how landlubbers wore them every day. She wiggled her feet into the sandals with distain, grabbed her bag, and left the room.

Four athletic-looking men waited by the elevator.

They eyed Luna like she was an appetizing morsel as they sniffed the air.

"Dinner" one jested. A short-lived wolf howl and snorted laughter followed the lewd jeer.

Another whistled and called out, "Dessert!"

While the young men snickered, Luna approached without trepidation. She was getting the hang of picking out the mundane from the others. She suspected this rowdy pack were shifters—wolves—the same rambunctious group she'd seen at dinner. Their magnified testosterone was meant to intimidate other males and excite females. Luna merely grinned at them. She had handled the vampire—she could handle these pups.

In the last two days, these wolf shifters had wandered around the island in T-shirts with similar hockey logos. They certainly looked like hockey players. Each one of them buff and a couple of them had crooked noses. Most likely, this rough gang came here to heal sports injuries. When the waters froze in the far north, she'd observed the sport from under the ice, witnessing several unforgiving high stick blows in her lifetime. To sirens, those men were always an option for sacrifice—enjoyable to mate and challenging to drown.

A chime dinged, capturing the group's attention, and the elevator door opened. Luna wandered in and turned to press the lobby button.

The pack tramped in and surrounded her.

"How about you join us for dinner?" said one guy with a crooked nose.

Meat eaters for sure. "Tempting, but I'll pass," she stated with mock regret.

The door reopened seconds later, and she seemed suddenly forgotten as the pack rushed out in front of her. Guessing the smell of cooked meat was a stronger draw for them, she trailed slowly behind the rollicking group.

The dining room hummed with chatter, and Luna's heart rate picked up when she paused. In the backroom, the only seats available were at the vampire's table. In the main room, her options were limited—she could sit with the blondes or the birdwatcher. While Luna contemplated her choices, one blonde suddenly elbowed the other, bringing her friend's attention to the entrance. Luna glanced over her shoulder in curiosity at their owlish eyes. At the sight of Nate, she instinctively moved to sit in the chair opposite the birdwatcher, Charlie. From the corner of her eye, she saw the skinnier blonde wave Nate over and offer him a seat. He sat with them, two tables away.

What do I care who Nate dines with? After their intimate encounter under the tree yesterday afternoon, she had suffered through dinner with him again last night. With every effort, she'd tried to remain aloof while Nate chatted and laughed in his easy manner. She'd pretended like nothing amazing—or mind-blowing—had occurred between them under the tree. Luckily, tonight, Charlie's table was small and set for two.

"Is something the matter?" Charlie asked.

Luna relaxed the scowl from her face and replaced it with a sweet smile. "I'm fine."

Distracted throughout dinner, she stumbled through conversation with Charlie. Every time she heard peals of laughter from the blondes, she cringed—and, when Nate chuckled, jealousy squeezed her heart. Before she'd come downstairs, she'd decided she would avoid Nate, so why had she taken the time to do her hair and slip into a sexy dress? The conflicting emotions drove her to distraction, bordering insanity.

What was it about Nate? He claimed she was his *mate*—but it was impossible! Her kind was destined to be alone. Even if she wanted him, if they mated anywhere near the water, the urge to drown him would be too great.

What are my options?

Glancing at the vampire, she recalled his advances the other night in the corridor. She could not drown what was already dead. The thought of pleasing him made her skin crawl, and the taste of spoiled fish filled her mouth. Her appetite gone, she pushed the plate away and excused herself.

"Good night, Charlie."

With Charlie's farewell over her shoulder, she skirted the table next to her. Luna cruised within an arm's length of the blondes' table where Nate remained seated. Proud of herself for not looking in his direction even once through dinner, Luna focused on the patterned carpet as she calmly maneuvered past the trio. Weakness shook her resolve. At the last moment, she glanced up. Nate's relaxed torso slunk casually in the chair, and their eyes met. His penetrating gaze probed her. Heat ignited in her belly, and her breath hitched.

With a shaky inhale, she rushed past him and barreled for the lobby. She desperately needed fresh air. *Is this what it feels like to drown?* Trembling, she continued past the front desk until she was outside. The salty wind tugged her hair, and she tilted her face upward for a healthy gulp of oxygen. Inhale. Exhale. Breathe.

Mildly pacified, she needed to release further tension, and nothing was better than being in the water. She'd only spent an hour swimming this morning during her session with Selena—the mermaid's words came flooding to her now. "There could be a life for you outside of the oceans, but you won't know unless you give the people in this landscape a chance. Especially here at the Wiccan Haus where there are a variety of beings to learn more about. Open your eyes and you'll start to see you are not alone."

Luna pulled off her sandals and stuffed them into her bag. The grass offered a welcomed and cool cushion under her feet as she padded along the hill. The stars winked in the indigo evening sky. Pondering the vastness of the universe made her feel small. *Where is my place? Where do I belong?* Unlike the other sirens, Luna never got used to the solitude of the immense oceans. At a young age, she'd moved into a palace above the water while her sister sirens made their homes in the caverns under the island. *Why am I so different than them? Why do I long to belong with someone when I know it's impossible? Is the water god responsible for the change in me? None of my sister sirens felt compelled to belong with a man.* Sure, they'd been delighted in acting like the water god's harem, but they didn't feel love for the god in the way she did. She had loved...and lost. *Can I love again? Should I?*

Now in possession of a normal heart rate, Luna paused in the clearing and crossed her arms over her chest. "You can stop following me, Nate."

Nate uncloaked and appeared before her eyes. It was a bit unnerving.

Seemingly perturbed, he held up his palms. "How did you know I was following you? Did you *see* me?"

"Not you exactly...more like a blur in your general shape. By the size of you, it was an easy assumption." Though she managed to recognize the vampires and the wolf shifters, she still wasn't certain about him. He could cloak, but she sensed something more.

"Hmm, disconcerting...unless it's because you're my mate. Mates often have unique bonds." His voice was hopeful.

"Nate"—she shook her head exasperated, tousling her hair—"it doesn't make sense. I can't be your mate.

I've lived in another realm my whole life, with the exception of occasionally visiting the human realm. We are different species. And yet, by chance, we've come together?" She shrugged. The odds were too great.

"It's how fate works best...when two unlikely souls meet. Things are cosmically set in motion to alter our paths. Remember why you came here. You left a relationship that wasn't meant to be. Give our relationship a try."

"I don't know." She looked up at the full moon—her namesake. It pulled at the tides within her.

"I have an idea. I know a place to hang out for a while so we can get to know one another." She opened her mouth to decline, but he raised his palms, stopping her. "They have games. Have you ever played pool?"

"Pool? Like swimming pool?"

"No. There is no water in this pool." He chuckled. He extended his hand toward her. "What do you say?"

Wow, I love when you smile.

Not only was he sexy as hell, but he was good-natured and fun to be around—exponentially upping the hot factor. Calling her his mate seemed too good to be true; if she wasn't careful, she could fall for him. She imagined giving in to her lust, picturing them kissing while she led him into the water. But it would be the same as before with mundane men—an overwhelming sensation of desire plunging deeper into bloodlust. It always consumed her. Those few experiences of killing left her sick, and she was grateful the god had replaced those men as her lover. She never let on to the other sirens how much the murders affected her.

I am different than them. She accepted her fate. Glad, really. *Maybe I can control the savagery in me?*

The god had a way of blocking her instinct to kill when they were intimate—she could just enjoy the pleasure they gave each other without guilt. But, here and now, she didn't know who or what Nate was exactly. If they were together in the water, she was terrified her desire and urge to kill would overpower everything else. Nate wouldn't likely survive their love tryst. Staring longingly at his palm, she guessed he would be safe if there was no *pool* of water.

"Do I have to wear my shoes?"

He glanced at her feet then burst out laughing. "Shoes are optional."

She slipped her hand into his and regretted how her heart fluttered. She accepted her previous, and only, relationship wasn't meant to be. Why jump from one man's arms into another's—no matter how strong and sexy those arms were? Wouldn't it be asking too much if her heart healed and loved again within a week's time? Her pride told her to stand on her water-god-given two feet.

While they strolled, Nate explained more about the game of pool. The idea of sinking a ball into a pocket by shooting it with a stick sounded tricky. He bragged how he often played at a pub near his home where he gave the locals a run for their money.

They entered a clearing surrounded by tall pines. In its center, a petite, white-washed cottage greeted them with cheery, bright lights glowing from within.

"Wow. How did you know about this place?" They had only been on the island a few days, and, just yesterday, Nate had been lost on his way to yoga.

"Myron, the receptionist, told me about it." He shrugged and, with a crooked smile, added, "It's known as the Fun Shack, so let's have some fun. Don't worry; it's bigger than it looks."

Hmm. He's been here before. Some things weren't adding up regarding her handsome date. Had she been too distracted and starry-eyed by his sexy-man magnetism to notice before?

Luna recalled seeing him the other day in the woods with the head of security and the owner of the

Wiccan Haus. When the men came out of the trees, catching up with her and Charlie, Nate had been there but cloaked. Why avoid being seen? Even now, her suspicions raised another notch when they entered through the squeaking screen door of the Fun Shack, and Nate smiled and waved at Rekkus. *Okay. They know each other, but for how long? Rekkus doesn't seem like the welcoming-committee type.*

The head of security acknowledged Nate before turning his attention to the woman across from him where the two sat at a table. Rekkus dropped his gaze to scowl at the board game lying between them. The dark-haired woman counted as she moved a tiny silver dog across the spaces. After her turn, she tilted her head and smiled warmly at Nate.

She recognizes him, too. Perplexed, Luna scanned the large room. Somehow, it appeared vastly larger on the inside than the outside—just like the Wiccan Haus lodge. Half the tables were occupied with people she hadn't seen before; perhaps they were staff members here to chill at the end of the day. Two guests she recognized sat at a table tucked against the window, concentrating over a chess set. A cracking sound caught Luna's attention. Brightly colored balls on a felt-covered table rolled in all directions. Immediately, she recognized the four athletic wolf shifters looming around the pool table. They simultaneously swung their heads in her and Nate's direction, sniffing the air. Their stares narrowed in on her.

Suddenly, Nate rubbed his arm against hers in an odd way, and then his hand reached up and caressed her bare shoulder. She gave him an annoyed glance and stepped away, but she failed to move beyond the reach of his long arm.

Under her breath, she tightly asked, "What are you doing?"

"I'm putting my scent on you." His rubbing would appear like a lover's caress to the human eye, but it was to ward off the wolves.

When her gaze cruised to the wolf pack, their attention shifted between her and Nate. Territory established, they avoided making further eye contact with Nate and returned to their game. One of them continued to leer at her. Earlier in the hotel elevator, he'd referred to her as *dessert*.

Still reprimanding Nate under her breath, she said, "You can't just stake your claim on me. I don't belong to you." *Yet, if I surrender to you as my soul mate, you would claim me—and I you.* At his hurt expression, she regretted her words and the tone in which she flung them.

"All right, Luna, the moon is full, and shifters are unpredictable under such conditions. I don't want any trouble for you."

Touched by his concern, she was glad her rash discouragement hadn't deterred him. Truthfully, now no longer protected by the water god, she found herself comforted by Nate's.

He dropped his grip from her shoulder, but captured her hand, flashing a devilish grin. She shook her head and stifled a laugh at his boldness. How did he easily melt her frozen heart and break her resolve?

Heavy footfalls shook the old floorboards as Nate maneuvered her to an adjacent table from Rekkus and the woman. The head of security called to Nate, stopping him in his tracks.

"Nate, why don't you and Luna join us?"

"Oh, you know my name?" *Why does the head of security know my name?* She remembered his from when he announced himself and Cyrus Rowan to her and Charlie outside the woods. *Cemil warned me not to sing. Maybe Cemil mentioned my being here to Rekkus? Beware a dangerous siren to be watched.* She couldn't help but stare at the man who studied her like shark's prey. Besides, he was also interesting to look at. *What are you?*

"I know the name of every guest—it's my job. Please, join us. This is my wife, Dana." Rekkus indicated the woman who offered a welcoming hello.

Nate pulled up two chairs, and they sat.

Dana turned to her husband. "Why don't we put the game aside and finish it later."

Rekkus grunted, unenthused. "Nate, join me at the bar, and we'll get some drinks."

"Yes, excuse us, ladies."

The large men rose, but Rekkus turned to his wife and asked, "Can I get you another cider?"

"No, I'm fine." Dana smiled at her husband, love shining in her eyes. Her gaze followed him and lingered for a moment as he sauntered away. She turned to Luna. "You should try the cider if you haven't already. It's made with fresh apples from the orchard on the island."

"Sounds great." Luna glanced at Nate who'd waited for her response.

He winked.

The gesture sent butterflies fluttering in her belly, but she didn't let it show on her face how he affected her. It was best if it looked like they were merely friends *or* perhaps guests who happened to walk in at the same time.

As the men crossed the room, Dana asked, "So, how do you like the Wiccan Haus?"

"It's a unique and magical place." Luna meant it, too.

Dana nodded. "Have you done some of the classes or treatments?"

While Luna shared her positive experience with Selena, her attention continued to drift to the tall man at the bar. Nate was always the tallest in the room. At one point, Nate and Rekkus were leaning in, heads close together, and they seemed to be in an intense discussion. When their drinks were ready, Nate pointed to the felt table before he picked up his glass. Rekkus collected two drinks and headed to their table. He handed one amber-colored glass to Luna, and then took a sip of the other, darker liquid. Nate crossed the room to where the werewolves played pool. He dug into his pocket and pulled out a palm of coins, which he then placed in a stack on the edge of the table.

"What's he doing?" Luna asked.

Rekkus briefly glanced over. "He's indicating he wants the next game. Do you play pool?"

"No, do you?" Luna glanced between them. She caught the sly look Dana gave her husband.

Rekkus shrugged. "From time to time."

Nate returned and slid into the chair beside her. "They're almost done." He tipped his head in the direction of the pool table. "Then, I will show you how to play."

Fifteen minutes later, her half-full glass forgotten, she stood with a narrow stick in her hand, running her fingers over the green felt.

"Stand back while I break," Nate said.

She retreated three steps. Nate leaned his sculpted body carefully over the table. With an impressively loud crack, the balls scattered, two sinking into pockets. She watched with interest while he sank two more.

"Okay, your turn. You shoot the solid color balls. Hold your cue like this." When she mimicked his hold, he said, "Good. Give it a try."

She glanced across the room at Dana and Rekkus, but they weren't watching. Instead, they'd returned to their board game. Time to choose a shot; Luna surveyed the felt field and the colorful orbs. Stalling, she tossed her mane of ebony hair over her shoulder and caught the eye of one werewolf. He was still ogling her like she was dessert. When she returned to her task, Nate was at her side.

"Here, lean in like this." He guided her against his warm body to bend over the table. Feeling her behind pressed against his hard leg made her lose focus. His lips at her hair, he said, "Aim for the red one, but hit the white one right here." His arm was wrapped around her, holding the cue stick, and he slightly forced the stick to almost tap the white ball to give her an exact target.

She clenched the pole in her hand and licked her dry lips. "I got it. Thanks." When Nate stepped off, the air instantly cooled around her. The shot she delivered knocked balls into other balls, her turn ended. It was unexpected how much she enjoyed the game—and Nate's company. She had to admit he'd lightened her spirits by making her laugh from his antics.

"You won!" He held up his hands in defeat.

"What? How could I have won with all my balls still on the table?"

"I scratched. If a player sinks the white ball while shooting at the eight ball, they automatically lose."

"Nate, you did that on purpose." She pressed her lips together and flared her nostrils in mock frustration.

"No, beautiful, you won fair and square. Do you want to play again?" He undressed her with smoldering eyes. She read what he wished to do instead of another game of shooting pool.

"I think one game is enough."

He flashed his teeth at her concession before they carried the pool cues to the hanging rack on the wall. Two of the four wolf shifters who played before them took the cues off their hands and started a new game. The other two shifters headed for the door.

Luna and Nate returned to the table where Dana was folding up the board game.

"Who won?" Nate picked up his glass and sucked down a healthy swallow.

"I did." Dana smiled.

"I didn't know you were into playing Monopoly. Isn't pool more your thing?" Nate raised an eyebrow at Rekkus and grinned. It was clear as day the man hated the long, drawn-out, and tedious game.

The large man shrugged. "My wife likes to play."

Rekkus was all hard muscle, discipline, and testosterone, but, when he looked at his wife, there was softness in his expression. Dana, smiling at him, knew she had it good. A wash of longing to belong to someone filled Luna, followed by a deluge of envy.

"So, you seem to know each other. Have you been to the island before?" Luna asked Nate.

"Yes, I was injured and came here to recover—but it was a long time ago." Nate shrugged one shoulder and downed the last of his drink. "Can I get anyone another drink?" He took drink orders and headed for the bar.

So, he confessed. However, she wanted to ask about his injury and if he was okay from it, but he'd slipped away, evading two of the many questions she had. *How did you get so chummy with a man like Rekkus if you'd stayed only once before? Why didn't you mention you have been here before? What was this mysterious injury? Who are you, Nathaniel Quinn?*

When he returned, the conversation flowed, but Luna got quiet. She plastered her charming, youthful smile to her face, but her mind raced as she examined Nate's every word and mannerism, trying to find clues. When the pool table freed, Nate invited Rekkus to play. Luna swore she saw Rekkus crack a smile.

"Do you mind if Dana keeps you company for a bit?" Nate leaned in close to her. "We can leave after this. Maybe go for a walk?"

"I'm fine. Good luck." Playing at this normalcy, two couples hanging out together gave her angst as she tried desperately to fit in. She found it difficult to relax and enjoy the time in this room, and, for that matter, her time here at the Wiccan Haus. She'd vowed to change, but she couldn't have accounted for a man who claimed they were fated mates—a man who sent her pulse racing every time he was near. When he suggested they leave together, spending more time alone, she couldn't think straight. It alerted her fight or flight instinct. She waited for Nate and Rekkus to engage in the game before she thanked Dana for a nice evening.

"Wait. You're leaving without Nate?" Dana's brows drew together.

"I'm getting tired. Could you tell him I'll see him tomorrow?"

"Um. Of course. It was nice meeting you."

"You, too." Luna followed Dana's glance toward Nate. The two men were engrossed in the game and what looked like playful banter. The room had filled over the past hour. Thankfully, she slunk out unnoticed.

Outside, the tang of the ocean teased her even this far inland. It mingled with the heavy scent of pine. She longed for a swim and so headed toward the lake. Meandering along the lane, lost in thought, she startled at the snapping of a large twig. She slowed her pace, scanning the darkness of the trees. A man dashed out from the woods, skidding on the gravel and blocking her way. Though forced to stop, Luna showed no fear.

"Well, well. I think it's time for *dessert*. Are you as sweet as you look?" asked the shirtless werewolf. His athletic body glistened with sweat in the filtered moonlight, and the hair around his ears hung in damp waves to his collarbones.

"I think you need to curb your sweet tooth before you lose your canines."

He guffawed at their exchange of witty banter. "Maybe you're right." He pretended to consider something. "Yeah, you know, ever since I smelled you in the elevator, I started craving salt. I bet your skin tastes salty."

"Why don't you come closer and find out?" Her voice was cool and clear as the night air around them.

Suspicious, the werewolf glanced around, his nostrils flaring. After a long and silent moment, he asked, "Where's your hairy friend?"

"Right. Here." The words, growled low and menacing, filled the woods.

"What the hell!" The shifter wildly sniffed the air, trying to pinpoint the threat. Suddenly, he froze and stared over Luna's head at the Sasquatch who uncloaked directly behind her.

She didn't turn around; she only crossed her arms over her chest with a huff.

The shifter held up a palm. "I was just out for a moonlit run. I'm leaving now." He turned tail and ran.

Luna pivoted and lifted her chin, meeting Nate's glower. She gulped. She'd never seen this hard, warrior before. The cords in his neck stuck out like tree roots. But still, his menacing, sobering demeanor wasn't going to deter her. "Nate—"

"Why did you leave without me? You never know who can be in these woods—especially on the night of a full moon."

"It's considerate of you to care, but you don't need to follow me around. I can take care of myself."

"What were you going to do? You're bound not to sing."

"Sing! How do you know?" she asked, stunned. "What did Cemil tell you? Is that why Rekkus watches me?"

Nate shrugged. "It's forbidden. No harm shall come to the guests at the Wiccan Haus. Besides, not all paras are so affected by your songs."

"Thanks for the slogan and the warning. And

singing isn't my only weapon." Being protected was a worthy notion, but his sneaky process bordered on overbearing. He'd pushed her to the point of no return. She felt undignified, but justified, with what she was about to do. In a swift motion, she unhinged her jaw, yawned impossibly wide, and exposed her razor-sharp teeth. Just as quickly, she snapped her mouth shut and swirled away.

She expected to hear him renounce his claim about them being fated mates. She couldn't face him—to see his appalled expression would be her undoing. However, he wasn't backpedaling.

"I know you are capable, Luna. It's just...."

She peeped at him over her shoulder when he hesitated.

He ran his hand through his hair. "I thought we were making headway. I thought you were having fun...and then I looked up to see you walking out the door." His cold, hard expression altered, and contrition filled his features.

A pang of guilt settled like a stone in the pit of her belly. "I did have fun. And I like spending time with you." She longed to reach out to him, but, instead, she'd bared her teeth, hoping to convince him she could protect herself and he'd be better off without her. But he witnessed her inner monster—it hadn't fazed him.

"Then what is holding you back?" he asked.

"I've belonged to another for so long, but I had to let go. It poisoned me." She sighed. "I just think I'm on a solo journey now. I wish it could be different."

"A solo journey is not your destiny."

She dropped her gaze to her dirt-covered toes with a heavy sigh, resolved not to continue the subject. "I'm going for a swim. Good night, Nate." She continued on the path but called over her shoulder, "Don't follow me."

Chapter Five

Nate couldn't wrap his mind around the fact Luna detected him when he cloaked. He'd been more careful this time while he tracked her to the lake. Earlier at the bar, when he'd told Rekkus how she had described *seeing* his shimmery form, the weretiger seemed impressed. He further shocked his friend when he revealed the siren was indeed his fated mate. Nate then argued Luna could not possibly be a threat to the Rowans.

The weretiger knew all too well the importance of finding your soul mate as his sat just across the room. He'd remarked, "Well, this is a new development."

As Nate wound down the path to the lake, he thanked the full moon for the brilliant, flooding light it provided. He inhaled. Her scent lingered, teasing him, and arousing his inner Sasquatch. She'd draped her dress across a bush near the lake. Grinning, he confirmed Luna had disappeared under the moonlit surface, naked. He uncloaked and removed his clothing. *I'll make myself known.* He dove into the water and swam splashy laps. For a while, he fantasized what it would be like making love to Luna, craving to touch and taste her tight, smooth body. Ten long and silent minutes passed, and the stubborn siren wouldn't surface. Weary of swimming, he strode naked from the tranquil water. The scent of human women mingled with hairspray and cosmetics. Stifled squeals pierced the air. Nate inwardly groaned.

Not these two again. I guess they didn't take the hint.

Throughout dinner, the two divorcées, who'd come to the island to celebrate a new beginning, did nothing but hit on him. They spewed one lewd comment after another, until one of them had finally said, "I think you should come to my room."

He'd been quick to respectfully decline.

"Yoo-hoo!" The blonde as thin as a sapling branch waved.

"Hi, Nate." The other blonde's voice rasped against his nerves.

The first one ran her palm over her large, stiff boobs as she licked her lips. "Oh, wow."

"Ladies." Nate nodded at them. They'd caught him buck-naked, cock at full attention. *Just how am I going to get out of this?* Suddenly, something splashed behind him. He twisted, scanning the surface for Luna.

There were only ringlets rippling outward in the otherwise calm water.

"What was that? You're not alone?" The raspy blonde pouted her lips.

"Um." Nate wondered at the sudden timing of the splash. Unquestionable, it was Luna. *Why make sound now? Do these human nymphs have something to do with it?* He couldn't stop where his train of thought was headed. *Maybe a little flirting would prove interesting.*

"It was nothing. I'm here all by myself." His voice carried over the reflective surface before he swiveled toward the blondes. "What are you two doing here?"

"Nate, you're so naughty. We came out here to skinny dip, too."

"Mind if I join you?" He flashed them his devilish smile, dimples and all. He sauntered into the lake giving them a fabulous view of his ass. Sinking to his shoulders, he waited.

They pulled away their clothes and dropped them on the ground. Bobbing their heads, silly grins on their faces, they moved closer to him. Muffled squeals of delight carried over the water.

After five minutes of flirting, he was ready to give up on Luna appearing. The pheromones these women gave off as they circled closer turned his stomach. Skinny blonde latched onto his hips and groped around for his erection. His cock's gusto had diminished some with their intrusion, but she had no trouble finding and stroking its length under the water.

"Oh, wow, it's everything I dreamed it would be. Boy, Nate, you don't disappoint." She giggled.

"Whoa! Easy." He sucked in a breath.

The thought of enjoying a ménage à trois skipped across his mind so quickly he pressed himself to consider the idea. The blood pulsed to his lowered half as it responded to the vigorous attention it received. His body may have reacted on autopilot seeking satisfaction, but his heart and brain were in sync that he wanted Luna—only Luna—to do the satiating. The backstroke of his long arms coasted him to shore while the skinny blonde held on to his rudder. She was utterly engaged and enthralled.

Luna, where are you? Shit! I need to get out of here!

As soon as his foot touched bottom, he stood, but the woman didn't let go of his cock. The cool air felt refreshing on his torso and ass, but skinny blonde was building heat with the friction of her hands. She pointed the tip of his cock at her mouth and parted her lips.

"Uh, wait a—" he groaned.

"Give me some!" The blonde with the floating tits elbowed her friend.

Both women were on their knees facing his hips while the water sloshed around his thighs. Skinny blonde reluctantly let go of what she was about to put in her mouth, harshly sighing. With a smug grin, the other moved in to clap her jumbo, floating tits together, sandwiching his girth between them.

Fuck! Already so blue-balled from fantasizing about Luna, he wondered, *Why can't I just relax and let these two relieve me?* But he knew the answer. He was done with empty sex the moment he'd found his mate. These women couldn't relieve him in the way he needed. He wanted Luna—a lifetime with Luna. There was no woman he wanted more than her—not even two women.

"Enough. Ladies, enough. I need you to let go."

It was like talking bats out of a cave. They weren't listening.

Skinny blonde had circled him and wound her ivy-like arms around his body, stroking his behind. He couldn't dislodge from these clinging vines whose moans drowned out his protests. Suddenly, their moans turned into screams. Both women splashed wildly, abandoning him as they ran for dry land.

"There *is* something in there! It cut me," one cried.

"Ohmygawd, it scratched me!" cried the other at the same time.

They both turned their asses toward the lake lit by moonlight. Blood oozed from the dark slashes branding their ass cheeks and dripping down their wet legs.

So Luna did care.

"Oh, that's got to hurt." Nate bit his lip, holding back the urge to laugh until he could continue. "You should have Sage examine those cuts. She's an amazing herbalist."

The women hastily gathered their clothing and dressed, gingerly slipping on their shorts.

The busty one paused and turned to him. "Aren't you coming with us?"

"Uh, no. I'm going to stay...have a look around. Make sure the water is safe." Nate tried to hide his delight by sounding authoritative.

The women exchanged glances.

"Suit yourself." The skinny one spun on her heels and grabbed her friend's arm.

As they huffed away, their commercial-cosmetic scent dissipated. Nate deeply inhaled the fresh night air. It was like cleansing his pallet after eating something distasteful. He closed his eyes and listened to the symphony of frogs, crickets, and nocturnal creatures rustling in the night. He didn't hear a sound from the water behind him.

Seconds ticked by. He waited.

"Your friends are leaving so soon?"

Nate smiled at the sound of Luna's sultry voice. He opened his eyes to scan the empty footpath where the blondes had scampered off minutes before. He eased farther into the water and sunk to his shoulders, covering his renewed excitement at her nearness. Luna floated closer to him than he'd thought because she had to hastily move aside to avoid contact when he'd stretched out his arms.

"The blondes were eager to become my friends, but I'd prefer the company of a sassy siren with long hair—long enough to wrap around my shoulders. And eyes so big I could get lost in them."

She pressed her lips together and shook her head. He took this opportunity to clasp her hand, underwater. She tried to yank it away, but it was easy to capture the curve of her hip and draw her to him.

He settled onto his knees with the water circling his biceps, drawing her closer still. The tip of his nose touched the rapid pulse at her throat.

"It didn't seem that way to me. It looked like you were enjoying yourself."

She's furious.

She was likely giving him her best scowl, even her delicate brows drew downward and her pouty mouth... Well, damn, his urge to kiss her grew so strong he had to press his lips together. Mistakenly, he glanced down, now captivated by her small, high breasts as they rose and fell with suppressed anger. The pink buds beckoned him to touch them. He darted his tongue out, wetting his lips in preparation.

He gnashed his teeth together in an attempt to stay in control. It was imperative he tell her how he felt. He didn't want to play more games. She'd shown by attacking the blondes she couldn't let them have him, and the fact she was still angry proved it further. He knew Luna heard his protests.

Luna had tensed in rage when those human floozies not only threw themselves at Nate, but they hadn't stopped assaulting him when he'd asked them to. She'd seen everything crystal clear from where she'd swum underwater. Why hadn't Nate used his manly woodsman strength to rip those leeches off and cast them aside? Fueled by outrage, she'd drawn back her lips—her inner beast emerged—and her sharp teeth had prepared to strike. Those women got off lucky. She could have bitten off a chunk of their behinds! Well, they were gone, and, now, Luna had the woodsmen all to herself. However, she willed herself to remain angry because, if any other feeling wedged its way in, she'd be in trouble. Again, her inner voice reminded her she was here to mend her broken heart. Be free. *Why is this man complicating things? Why am I letting him?*

"Luna, don't you feel it?" His voice vibrated against her breastbone. "From the moment I first saw you, I felt the connection. And it's only grown stronger and stronger every moment from then on. Once I bond with my soul mate, we will be mates for life. Luna, you are my heart's desire, and I want you in my life...in my bed...."

She'd spent centuries with the water god thinking she was his soul mate, but the water god never claimed nor hinted she was his. He never promised her anything, not his undying love, devotion, or gratitude for all she had done for him. Yet, in a couple of days, this man had taken her existence to the next level. His glances from across the room had thrilled her. The heat from his hands on her skin excited her. But she fought it. She was bound not to sing, not to lure the island's occupants to their death, so, therefore, no love interaction on her part. She accepted the terms. Just because she was mysteriously attracted to this man, she would have to ignore it. The only problem was he wanted her—a siren. And she didn't have to sing to see it in the depths of his eyes. It signaled clear and true.

He is a fool for following me into the lake. "You should stay away from me. I'm dangerous."

"More so than vampires or witches? Can you cast a spell over me?" Humor and passion lit his eyes.

Raw emotion lodged in her throat, her eyes swam with tears threatening to spill out. "You wouldn't understand—"

"What Luna? That you're a siren?"

You are just a siren. Those were the hurtful words the water god had uttered when he made her see she would never mean more to him than the new woman in his life. Being a siren—she—hadn't been enough for the water god. Buried feelings of insignificance resurfaced, and she couldn't bear being rejected again.

"Damn it, Nate, I will drown you. I won't be able to control myself. It's the way of my kind," she cried desperately.

"Oh, honey, it would never happen." He cupped her soft cheek.

"Get your paws off me!"

His empathy fanned the anger raging almost unchecked inside her. She didn't want his pity any more than she'd wanted the water god's when he dismissed her love and devotion and chuckled at her naïveté.

Nate's hand remained clamped on her waist, the other hooked behind her slim neck. He refused to release her, sending her heart soaring—and plummeting—knowing he wouldn't let her leave. *What am I to do?*

"Please.... You're a fool to underestimate a siren's warning." She hung her head in defeat.

He brushed his lips across her forehead. "Don't let history define you. Look at me after all; I'm a Sasquatch with immense strength, tracking skills, and the ability to camouflage—great for a soldier—but not my calling. I'm happiest at my home in the northern woods with my dogs. I may serve when duty calls, but I make room in my life for more. I want a future with my mate."

A Sasquatch! The legend of Bigfoot. She'd only heard of the species and the unremarkable legend of their hunted existence. Placing her slim hand on his hairy chest, half out of the water, she stroked the long, dark strands, now drying and springing off his hard flesh. "Wow, I never would have guessed. Do you change...shift?"

He suddenly seemed disappointed, perhaps by her words or her tone. "I shift into the images of legend, when necessary. Does that repulse you?"

She winced like she'd been stung by an electric eel at the pain in his voice. Her breathing increased as her mind scrambled to fix this sudden change in him. His vulnerability gripped her at her core. *Are you my true mate for real—no tricks or spells?* Every fiber of her being screamed, "Yes!"

The plains of his chest were unyielding under her fingertips as they rose up until her hand held the thick column of his neck. "No—on the contrary—I want you more than anything."

He nuzzled his nose in the crook of her neck and pressed his lips to her throbbing pulse. "Luna, kiss me."

Sounds of pounding surf rushed her ears as his

soft lips beckoned her. She was a lost sailor on a cloudy night without a compass—Nate was her beacon. He brushed her lips with his, enticing. She desired more...more intimacy...more glorious feelings of being cherished and loved. The iceberg in her heart was melting.

She still doubted this man could truly love her—not even a god could.

He will know me—intimately—and he will pay dearly for it.

Swooping her mouth onto his, she fueled her kisses with strong and urgent passion. He responded by locking his arms around her, sealing her flesh to his. He slanted his mouth, deepening their kiss and plunging his tongue. She instinctually circled his tongue by tightening her lips around it and sucked hard, sliding it in and out of her mouth. A low, muffled growl rumbled in his chest as he stroked her flesh. The rhythm intensified her heat. When she pulled back to gulp in air, he cupped her face, forcing her gaze to his. No one had ever looked at her like Nate did. And something shifted inside of her.

"I want you, Luna." He must have seen the expression change on her face because he continued, "Why does it surprise you? You are beautiful, smart, interesting…and I could taste you for eternity."

She forced a swallow and drew her thighs together, indeed ready for him to taste her salty heat. "You don't know me. You will regret choosing me." She searched his face for understanding. "I've done things. People get hurt around me, Nate. I don't want to *hurt* you." *Kill you.*

He released her face and slid his fingers lower, spanning the milky white skin above her breasts. His palms glided over her nipples, firing a quiver down her spine. When his palms cupped her breasts and gently squeezed, she sucked in a jagged breath along with her bottom lip. The lip caught between her teeth felt tender and swollen. His gaze never left her face, seemingly content to watch her changing expressions as his thumbs brushed her nipples.

Her heart always flip-flopped at his wolfish smile.

"I'll take my chances. Do your worst, siren." Nate's head dipped, and his hot mouth captured the bud.

He'd remained on his knees during their kisses. Luna clutched the wild mane of his hair, squeezing the water from it. The droplets trickled down her silky arms. His mouth returned to hers, hungry. He stood, lifting her so she could wrap her legs around his waist. She sat, secured on the size of him between her legs.

His erection stretched beneath her junction, between the roundness of her ass and beyond. So, Nate was a match for a god.

She broke the kiss to speak but had to take a few shallow breaths first. His mouth didn't break contact with her skin. He ran hot kisses over her flushed cheeks, along her jaw, and skimmed her jugular with his teeth. This last action undid her. She was completely ready for him.

"Let's get out of the water," she said shakily.

"No."

"Please, Nate, it's safer."

"No."

"I can't promise—"

"Only promise to be my mate." He held her tight, drawing his head up to gaze at her. "Say yes, Luna. We *are* meant to be together."

A tear slid from her eye, shocking her. Rarely had tears filled her eyes, but never before had she shed them. More curiously, it made a sound when it hit the water. She knew her tears weren't for the loss of her water god because he didn't matter anymore. This tear was for Nate—for what she would do to him—because she nodded and said *yes*.

"Luna, allow me to claim you. And you me."

"Yes, Nate."

She pulled his mouth down to hers. She closed her eyes to ward off the army of advancing tears. The cool, night air caressed her skin until he moved them into deeper water. *Too deep!* His large hands gently lifted her buoyant curves to adjust her for his entry. He pushed against her opening, rousing her killer instincts. She refused to be like her sisters and wouldn't let the bloodlust control her. It had been so long since she'd been intimate with the god, or anyone. The savage return of her bloodlust scared her. It was too late to stop now. She'd said yes—and damn it—she meant it!

Gripping her hips with gentle force, he eased in, stretching against the soft tightness of her. He paused and let out a long, low breath, the strength of it blowing the hair around her ear. The sensation caused her to shiver. In turn, she shimmied lower onto his cock.

Is the joining of soul mates, especially during the first time, always this powerful and intense? She'd never before experienced anything like it—it seemed her very soul joined with his at a higher level of consciousness.

A shallow groaning from him began as a hum at

first, but it turned deeper—more menacing. He began
to rock, and she intuitively arched, matching his
rhythm. Her genetics were programed to pull him
under the water. The urge was as strong and extreme
as the spike drove her passion to the brink. It coiled in
her belly, a building of tension. It thrilled and terrified
her all at the same time. She whimpered as she let go,
allowing her body and soul to belong to this man. As
earthshattering as her climax was, after she reached
her pinnacle, her urge to kill him escalated. A melody
filled her mind. She inhaled a singer's deep breath, and
the lyrics died on her lips.

No. I won't do it. I won't kill him.

Elated she'd won, she clutched him to her, kissing
him wildly until he pulled away burying his face in the
wet folds of her hair. For a fraction of a breath, she
thought she felt a ruffle of fur under her fingertips as
Nate roared against her shoulder with one final thrust.

Under the moonlight, when his lips returned to
hers, the kisses were lingering and gentle. "Luna, I am
yours. And you are mine."

You are mine. The words floated around her head
while she wound her arms around his neck. However,
bloodlust overpowered any contentment.

At odds with her very being, she buried her

shaking hands in his hair. *No! It doesn't matter that you are my mate. I cannot transform like Selena. I tried. If I can't change for you, then I will never change.* Monumentally, she fought to clamp her jaw tight, but it seemed impossible to control the resurfacing urges in the water. *I won't bite him—maim his beautiful body.* Instead, she buried her devastation, a firestone sinking in her belly, and resolved to remain calm and in control. Sirens had cold hearts after all. Still, she forced their mouths together and guided him under the water, counting on her strength to amplify and his life ending quietly. *I'm so sorry, Nate, but I can't fight it anymore.*

Though Nate's eyes were still open, she guessed he probably couldn't see her well in the darkness. She, however, could see perfectly in the darkest depths. At war with herself, she fought both her powerful urge to drown him and her thoughts to save him, to love him. *This is who I am. A siren. He was so sweet to want me for the rest of his life. Only he didn't believe his life was going to end so soon.*

He didn't fight when she pulled him deep under the surface. The consuming bloodlust fueled her to drag him deeper. She hadn't sung to get him here, but, after his death, she would have to leave the island. A wave of remorse overwhelmed her. *I thought I was different.* She trembled with self-loathing.

Suddenly, Nate lifted her out of the water.

She blinked. He had easily broken away from her clutches. At the surface, flabbergasted, she sputtered, "How did you...? How can you...?"

He effortlessly carried her from the lake. "You will never physically overpower me, Luna. The power you have over me is in an entirely different way."

Elated by this news, she relaxed in his arms. She didn't—couldn't—kill him. Fate smiled on her after all. Nate broke her barriers and toppled her world. Now, he was her mate for life.

"You felt amazing. I almost lost control. I almost shifted while inside you." He looked relieved. "I've never felt like that before."

Lost control. Ha. I tried to kill you!

Still stunned, she couldn't keep from grinning at him while they dressed. He reached for her, and she walked hand in hand with him to the Haus. Under the gazebo, one of the blondes and the vampire who'd approached Luna earlier were making out. She elbowed Nate, alerting him to the couple. "If either of those blondes touches you again, I will bite off their fingers."

Nate chuckled.

Luna caught the vamp's eye. *Bite her good!*

Chapter Six

Luna strolled toward the Haus after her morning session with Selena, renewed and content. She searched for Sage to inquire about one of her famous shakes. Cemil had mentioned his sister made the best concoctions on the island, and, earlier today, Selena recommended them as well.

When she reached the lobby, the Zen atmosphere had changed. Luna paused. Several feet away, the ample-chested blonde she had seen groping the vampire last night—after groping *her* mate—raised her voice at Rekkus and Cyrus. Others hung around to listen, including Charlie, who leaned heavily on his cane. She proceeded to the front desk. Rekkus tapped information in a handheld device while the woman prattled on about her complaint. Cyrus casually strolled away, apparently allowing the head of security to handle the distraught woman.

"And where are these bites you woke up with?" Rekkus asked.

"Everywhere! My neck, my thighs, my tits. And I'm telling you it was that guy. I don't remember his name, but the pale one...you know, the one who could use a suntan."

Luna suppressed a laugh. Blondie got what she deserved after touching Nate. *The vampire is forgettable, but he did a lousy job glamouring you.* She stepped up to the counter and smiled at Myron. The ladies exchanged pleasantries as if nothing odd was occurring, though they heard every word.

"I'll file your complaint, and we'll have it rectified by this evening," Rekkus robotically informed the agitated woman.

"This evening! Why can't you just talk to the pervert now?"

Luna glanced their way. *Because he's a vampire who prefers the night.* She flicked her gaze to Myron. "Where can I find Sage? I was hoping to sample one of her famous smoothies."

"Sage usually works in the garden at this hour." The receptionist slid a paper forward and pointed to a drawing of its location on a trifold map.

"Perfect. Thank you."

Myron returned to flipping cards. Luna discreetly scanned the room. Many onlookers had moved out of hearing distance. Even Cyrus walked outside with Charlie, engaged in conversation. Heading out of the building, and feeling a little sorry for Rekkus, she couldn't resist one last glance at him.

"We have protocol and procedures." Rekkus glanced at his military grade watch. "If you have more to add, we can step into my office."

"Oh, there's more! I think you may need to drain the lake."

His gaze lingered on the entrance, making Luna wonder why Rekkus still seemed suspicious when he watched her leave. Did he think she might have something to do with the lake? Dashing into the sunshine, she skirted the building and found Sage in the garden.

After a pleasant fifteen-minute conversation with Sage, Luna left the herbalist to her task of tending the garden. Sage had offered to make her a shake right away, but Luna assured her there was no rush and she was headed for the beach to swim.

While the other guests congregated at a sandy beach, Luna preferred to bask on the smooth flat surfaces of the rocky shore on the other side of the island. She padded barefoot down the overgrown path toward the surf. An agonized moan filtered through the thinning trees. She halted and scanned her surroundings. It came again. Stepping off the path, she picked her way through the underbrush to investigate. A few hundred yards in, the owner of the Wiccan Haus, Cyrus Rowan, lay sprawled and semi-conscious in the vegetation. Her heart raced, and she gasped as she dropped to her knees beside him.

What possibly could have brought down this large man?

She leaned closer. A dart of some sort stuck out of Cyrus's neck. Instinctively, she plucked it out and tossed it aside. The puncture wound swelled, turning a blackish purple. Crashing footsteps penetrated the fog of bewilderment gluing her focus on Cyrus. Awareness infiltrated, and she pinpointed the culprit. Charlie ran away. She tried to solve this puzzle as her mind spun.

Charlie is running? Where is his walking stick?

She staggered to her feet, calling his name. He paused and narrowed his wild eyes at her. When she advanced toward him, she stepped on a hard object— Charlie's walking stick. She bent to retrieve the broken stick, except it wasn't broken. It lay in two pieces with a hidden compartment just large enough to contain something narrow like the dart.

Charlie must have shoved the dart into Cyrus's neck. A part of the puzzle solved, she exclaimed, "Charlie, what have you done!"

He bolted. She chased after him. *He's remarkably fast for a man with a bad knee.* As more puzzle pieces snapped into place in her mind, she realized birdwatching had been a disguise, and Charlie was an imposter. *But why? Why attack Cyrus?* She should have guessed he wasn't genuine when he hadn't recognized the common goldfinch. And she'd caught him spying on Cyrus in the woods several days ago. As the sticks poked at her feet, she grumbled, knowing she couldn't catch up to him. But she couldn't let him get away with this! There was only one thing she could do.

Taking a huge, shaky inhale, she exhaled in song.

***

The early morning hours had started with glorious lovemaking. Everything he'd heard about finding and connecting to a mate was astonishingly true. The worst part about it, though, was separating from her—he to his security duties and she to her session with Selena. Nate had hastily dressed, dragging his gaze from Luna's tempting, lithe body curled in the scattered sheets. Her black hair, long and luxurious, cascaded over the pillow in stark contrast to the snowy white linens. He'd blown a long, exaggerated breath to ease the tugging in his loins. Nate had other responsibilities and couldn't neglect the ongoing investigation into the death threat on Cyrus's life. As he reached for the doorknob, he'd stolen one final look at his mate before he left the room.

Nate's first order of business this morning would be informing Rekkus and the Rowans about what occurred regarding the wolf shifter and Luna last night under the full moon. The stunt the alpha pulled on the path had left him silently seething. Now Nate was bonded to Luna, his instincts to protect her surged, rivaling his instincts to love her.

He entered the security office and met Rekkus's serious gaze. He'd left the weretiger in the middle of an interesting pool game last night when he'd rushed out after Luna. Rekkus didn't comment about it, showed no emotion that anything unusual had occurred. Rekkus promptly started the meeting. As an added member to the security staff's morning meeting, Nate explained the incident.

He insisted after his monologue, "It would be my pleasure to handle the reprimand."

Nate and Rekkus had worked together several times in the past, and they were friends. Rekkus took a split second to respond. He gave a curt nod in agreement before moving on to other business.

Nate didn't need Cemil's tactful reminder. "Let's not forget or underestimate the pull of a full moon. Not all shifters can handle it. After all, some come here just for such reason—to help them deal with the unruly and sporadic emotions."

Every month, the morning following the full moon, the Rowans gathered to assess the issues that arose—there seemed to always be something. Placing humans and paras together during a full moon had its challenges. Nate and Rekkus exchanged glances. They knew well the call of the moon.

Nate left the security office and worked up in his mind how the pack could pose as a great threat to Cyrus; perhaps they were in on a conspiracy. While he puzzled all the angles, he made haste to the spa. Myron had tipped him off. The hockey players were receiving physical therapy treatments for their sports injuries. The four of them gathered in a relaxation room with an attendant placing ice packs on their swollen elbows and shoulders. When he entered, filling and disturbing the relaxation space, the tension in the room ignited. The alpha jumped from his lounge chair, his shoulders flexed and erect. The others sat up straighter, their jaws clenched. The nervous attendant whisked from the room and softly closed the door behind her.

Straight away, the alpha lowered his eyes, followed by his shaggy head in submission—this being the hardest thing for an alpha. His pack followed suit, giving the hulking Sasquatch respect.

Nate exhaled; his instincts told him these men were not a threat to Cyrus Rowan. And now the full moon cycle had passed, nor were they a threat to others. He followed up with standard questioning to be sure and learned the alpha was here to treat his full moon-induced, impulsive-control disorder. Nate recommended further treatment before he returned to the security office, neglecting to dish out punishment at the sincerity in which the alpha declared his apology.

Trekking to the Haus, he shrugged off his disappointment. There was nothing complicated to report. He'd hoped to close this mystery shrouding Cyrus's current threat, if only to dissolve and permanently remove the suspicion from Luna. Thoughts of her tugged and twisted his gut. His need to be constantly close to her and protect her surprised him. The height of the sun told him she should be back from her session with Selena by now. He quickened his pace, eager to lay his hands on her again.

Entering the lobby, he glanced about, hoping to spot his mate. He hid his disappointment behind the smile he flashed at Myron. However, Myron's stricken expression suddenly sent his hackles to attention. She blinked at him then returned her gaze to her scattered cards. Her resourceful card reading remained an important and reliable asset to the Rowans. While Myron hastily collected, shuffled, and flipped the cards again, Nate approached the security office. He intercepted Rekkus leaving the room with the same blonde woman who'd molested him last night in the lake. Her face was flush with anger, and she glared at Nate with supreme disappointment before she huffed away toward the elevators.

Rekkus didn't give the woman another moment of his time; instead, he looked down at his tablet. "Fucking vamps," he muttered in quiet frustration.

Nate recalled seeing the woman with a vamp last night. "What happened?"

"The bloodsucker didn't glamour her all the way and didn't cover up his marks."

"I think she was willing at least." Nate bristled at the thought of her touch.

"No doubt." Rekkus strode across the lobby. Nate

quickened his steps to keep the pace. "Sage is making her a mixture to keep her sleepy until the vamp is available to fix his lazy mistakes." Rekkus focused on his tablet.

"What's the big hurry?"

"I'm looking for Cyrus," Rekkus said. "He's not responding to the com."

Myron rushed over, gripping her hands tightly together. "Cyrus is in trouble!"

Nate knew the implication. With a potential assassin roaming the island, Cyrus was supposed to remain under watch at all times. "I'll help you look."

Rekkus tossed Myron his tablet and tapped the closed network com in his right ear, initiating a widespread search for their boss. Nate joined Rekkus's sprint.

After searching the immediate grounds, they spread out farther.

Outside, the familiar squealy squeaks of his red squirrel drew his attention. It occurred to him he hadn't seen the little guy in a couple days. The squirrel zigzagged in the direction of the cliff, which was odd because he normally stayed close to the tree line. Rekkus circled around and, when Nate caught his attention, he pointed toward the cliffs. Nate kept pace next to Rekkus as they raced onward. The squirrel ruffled its red tail and jumped across the grass toward the safe gardens surrounding the Haus.

Standing twenty-five feet above the rocky beach, Nate angled his glance over the cliff. Rekkus leaned over beside him. Nate shook his head in disbelief. Luna and Charlie were below. Rekkus let out a groan as a faint song floated on the breeze. Luna led a dazed Charlie in a hypnotic dance around boulders scattered in the sand toward the open sea.

Nate's heart thudded in his chest. *Why is my mate singing to this mortal?* It went against everything they had just shared. They'd mated so she was free from her siren's life and that very act. Not to mention, she was bound not to utter a melody while on this island. Still, his worst fear was she'd done something to Cyrus Rowan, proving to be a hired killer. A sudden pounding in his ears grew louder and more powerful than the surf below.

"Luna! Stop singing," Rekkus yelled into the wind, his roared words scarcely penetrating the drumming in Nate's ears.

Startled, Luna stopped and jerked her gaze up. Relief flooded her expression. Hope bloomed inside him until Rekkus's irate growl drew his attention. The weretiger hadn't liked she was here in the first place. He'd complained from the start she was dangerous, and the fact she came out of nowhere the day the ferry arrived had put him on red alert. Rekkus put his mate, Dana, and the Rowans first. Nate's friendship only extended so far—as did the fact he'd sacredly mated with Luna.

Damn, she is proving him right. Here she is singing and luring this man into the waves, but why?

"Oh, thank the gods! Hurry, Cyrus needs you!" Luna frantically pointed to the left beyond the rocks into the trees.

Everything happened quickly. Nate lifted his nose in the direction she pointed, but Rekkus must have picked up Cyrus's scent first because he shifted into his glorious seven-hundred-pound black tiger form and raced for the tree line, his silver stripes blurring in the brilliant sunlight. Rekkus's shredded clothes and boots tumbled in the grass.

"Charlie, put the needle down!" Luna exclaimed.

At the fury in her voice, Nate's attention shot to the scene below. Charlie had awakened from his trance and now held a large, pointy needle with a feather base, similar to a tranquilizer dart, in his fist. Nate suspected it was something more lethal. Cold fear coiled in his abdomen. Luna dashed to the right, but Charlie countered her movements. For every calculated step Luna took, Charlie stayed at equal distance, holding the dart at the ready. Nate assessed the situation twenty-five feet below the cliff.

Every fiber of his being raged. He let out a deafening roar. It echoed in the air around him before he leaped. Nate shifted in midair, unleashing the hairy beast, the Sasquatch, as claws extended from his fingertips and his strength amplified.

The startled birdwatcher swiveled just in time to be pounced on, and then Charlie was slammed flat on his back against a nearby slab of rock, knocking his head with force. Charlie swooshed out a harsh breath accompanied by a howl of pain. Struggling and dazed, he lifted his head slightly to look at his right arm— bloody and pinned to the stone. Nate's claws had nearly severed it to the bone. The poisoned dart toppled from his outstretched, trembling fingers. It clanked in the pebbles.

Charlie rapidly lost blood, and so, wouldn't be going anywhere. Threat contained.

The air rang when Nate retracted his claws, and they scraped against the rock. He shifted, sweat dripping from his brow. Blood covered his throbbing fingers, and his pores were pinked from the shift. His clothes were split at the seams.

Nate's gaze rolled to Luna as he stood. She inched closer, looking wild and beautiful with flush cheeks and the wind in her hair. He searched her face—did those large, fathomless eyes seem repulsed? He'd shifted into his other form, mistimed by forced rage, and revealed to her his true beast. Failing to display this side of himself before now could cost him his mate. He swallowed a remorseful gulp. *If only I had shifted earlier under controlled conditions. I should have shown her before we mated.*

She offered him a grateful, understanding smile. Supreme relief filled him. His mate accepted him for who he was. Danger past, Luna flung herself in Nate's waiting arms. He held her and stroked her wind tangled hair with one hand, careful not to get blood on her.

"Charlie shot Cyrus with one of those darts. I think it's poisonous. Cyrus was incoherent when I came upon him in the woods off the beach path."

"It's all right; Rekkus will get to him in time. Are you hurt?"

She didn't appear to be shaken up, though he was haunted by the what-ifs, which prompted him to kiss her temple.

"I'm fine. I'm so glad you and Rekkus made it here in time. I didn't realize Charlie had another dart until he came out of his trance. He must have had it in his pocket." She tilted her head sideways, glancing at the weapon lying atop of the colorful pebbles.

Nate was profoundly grateful she'd followed her instincts.

"There was no other way to overpower him without...singing...bringing him into the water. After he was no longer a threat, I was going to come for help."

"I understand." He pressed further kisses to her brow. "You did what you thought was best."

With Luna safe, he turned his attention to another matter. *Did Rekkus find Cyrus in time?* Nate released her and adjusted his stance, scanning his surroundings. He collected the dart then stepped away from the moaning man. He thought his roaring must have alerted security to their location or perhaps Rekkus called in backup. Either way, voices filtered down from the cliff top. He squinted skyward. Cemil's fair hair waved in the breeze against the blue sky, a tactical team surrounded him.

"Initiate operation 742," Cemil said.

The squad leader repeated the command in his headset, directing men to the beach. The team jogged off in the direction Rekkus had raced and soon came down the path to the shore. They dressed Charlie's arm and took him into custody. Another soldier confiscated the dart.

Commands were shouted from the cliff top. Returned to human form, carrying an unconscious Cyrus, Rekkus came into view. A security team member slung a standard issue foil blanket around Rekkus's naked shoulders. Another collected his tattered clothes and boots, leaving no evidence behind. Over their heads, a loud and flashing thunderstorm kicked up out of nowhere as the team moved out. Nate guided Luna to the Haus.

The two Rowan sisters, Sage and Sarka, met them inside the entrance. The lobby, emptied of guests, was a welcome sight. The eldest sister Sarka directed Rekkus and the troop through a doorway. Cemil had been clutching his brother's arm as he'd trekked along beside Rekkus. Cemil released his grip at the doorway and faced Nate and Luna.

"Thank you, Luna. We got to him in time. Sarka will help him." Cemil glanced up at Nate and placed his hand on his shoulder.

Nate tensed. He sensed Cemil reading him.

Cemil's glance flickered to the blood drying on Nate's hand. "You are uninjured. We will keep you informed about Cyrus, but, for now, your mate should be your priority. Now the assassin has been identified, you are relieved from duty."

Shit. Thanks for your discretion. Nate shot an anxious glance Luna's way. She didn't return his gaze, only stared intently at Cemil. The lie about Nate only being a guest was another untimely reveal.

Cemil spun away and closed the door. Luna turned large, question-filled eyes at Nate.

Heh, sirens aren't known for their forgiving hearts. "Let's go to your room. There are some things I need to tell you."

They rode the elevator in silence. When they entered Luna's room, she crossed to the window. Nate slipped into the bathroom to wash the dried, sticky blood off his hand. He returned to find she hadn't moved.

With a hollow sound to her voice, she said, "The storm has passed. The sky is clear again. Isn't it odd a storm blew in just when they carried Cyrus inside?"

Nate shook his head, glancing out at the sunny sky. "Operation 742. It's a spell designed to resemble a lightning storm. It charges the air with magic to help shield things from humans. It also sends them running inside for cover, though several rooms, like the lobby, are infused with magic to keep them clear. Most humans don't see what they aren't supposed to see—their brains shut out what shouldn't be there, but, under extenuating circumstance, the storm helps the effect a bit."

Luna listened, but her stiff shoulders and jutting chin marked her suspicion. "How exactly do you know all this, Nate? And Cemil said you are relieved from duty. What does that mean?"

He couldn't hide the truth any longer. He crossed his arms, toying with the holes along the seam of his T-shirt. "I didn't come here for a vacation. I was called to duty by the Syndicate, a governing body who rules the para species, because there was a credible death threat tip-off on Cyrus Rowan's life. The man has a bounty on his head. Though Rekkus is his bodyguard, as well as the head of security for the Wiccan Haus, I was called in to go undercover. Many years ago, I was drafted by the Syndicate and fought for two decades against the paranormal beings who threaten human lives. During which time, I sustained injuries after taking out a coven of vampires. I came here to heal. I wouldn't have survived in an ordinary military hospital." He couldn't meet her eyes and focused on another lengthy split in the seam.

"So you knew there was someone coming to the island to assassinate Cyrus?"

"Yes. They have a high-tech screening process, but paras find their way around new tech all the time. That's why you were immediately under suspicion when you showed up with no reservation— conveniently taking the spot of a guest who unexpectedly canceled."

"Oh!" She glanced out the window, a sad, faraway expression crossing her face. "It's why you followed me from the start?"

"Luna, I...." He paused. "Rekkus assigned me to tail you, but I never suspected you. And it's no lie we are fated mates." He cozied up to her and took her hand, tenderly squeezing it. "Luna, please, look at me." She tilted her head, and her eyes glistened with unshed tears. Fear of rejection burned in his gut. "You know it's true, right? I am yours, you are mine."

"I know." Her voice quavered, and her love shone brightly among the teardrops clinging to her lashes. "I understand why you couldn't tell me before about your assignment. And this explains a lot, but is it everything?"

"Yes, I'm not trying to leave anything out. Do you have more questions?"

She shrugged, grinning through the tears. "I can't think of any at the moment."

"Are you okay with this, then? Do you forgive me? Because I will never keep things from you again."

She nodded as she examined his face, her searching, soulful eyes dark as caves. He waited for her to say more. After a long moment, the lines disappeared between her brows, and her mouth curved into a smile. "Earlier when you shifted...well...I thought you were hairy before."

Mirth filled him, and he chuckled. She'd made light of his full-out Sasquatch form—hair, teeth, claws, and all. She'd shown her additional teeth last night, expecting to warn him off, but he would love her no matter what. It seemed their hidden talents were on the table, and they had no more secrets to hide. The fact he'd nearly lost her heightened his need for her. If she'd been pricked with the poison dart, would his little siren have survived? The capsule held a seemingly hefty, lethal dose. Cyrus Rowan was a large man in comparison.

He took her face in his calloused palms and

brushed his lips against hers. She clutched him to her. He deepened their kiss and continued at a frenzied pace as he tugged her clothes off. His soon followed. He settled her against the mattress, sinking her under his weight. Mouths joined with bruising pressure and urgency, Nate swiftly entered her folds. Luna wiggled and bucked, conforming to his size. With their legs intertwined, he grunted against her with each thrust until she broke the kiss to cry out. It was sweet music to his ears. Her warm sheath spasmed around him, pushing him over the edge, and his control shattered. With one final thrust, he filled her. The intensity of his climax left him panting and damp with sweat. He clung to her in silence and reverence. She rested her arms around his shoulders and caressed the damp locks of his hair. After his heart rate returned to normal and his body cooled, he moved to the shower, taking Luna with him for a slower, more involved, performance.

Dinner hour approached, and the couple dressed. Luna groaned when she put on her sandals. "Why do people wear these things?"

Nate chuckled. "Those aren't even high heels. Mmm, I bet you'd look amazing in high heels and nothing else." He grinned at her and wiggled his eyebrows.

She ignored his comment. "Couldn't I go barefoot...or not at all?"

"I'll let you in on a little secret. Dinner is mandatory because the Rowans need a daily head count. They can't be careless with vampires and the like prowling around. Right?"

Luna agreed by shuffling to the door. "Okay, fine, I'm ready."

Exiting the elevator downstairs, Nate called to Cemil who stood in the lobby, "Evening." When he was within elbow distance, he asked in a lower voice, "How is everything?"

"Good evening. Won't you both join my siblings and me in the office for a few minutes before you head to the dining room?"

"Of course." Nate glanced reassuringly at Luna, despite his apprehensive curiosity. He hadn't forgotten Luna had broken her contract. He followed Cemil inside with Luna close to his side.

Rekkus, fully clothed, stood by the window with his arms crossed. Sage stood beside her sister's chair. Sarka, regally seated, reigned behind a wooden desk. Cemil offered them seats and leaned against the desk.

Nate focused on Sarka. Her hair, dark like Cyrus's,

was piled on top of her stately head and secured by two pencils. Sarka and Cyrus were referred to by the staff as the dark ones while Cemil and Sage were called the light ones, likely because of their golden heads of hair and friendlier personalities. The four siblings shared the same vivid, ice-blue eyes and aristocratic good looks.

Cemil indicated the woman behind the desk. "Luna, this is my eldest sister, Sarka." He swept his arm in Luna's direction. "Sarka, this is Luna."

"Hello," Luna said.

Sarka nodded.

Nate already knew her, of course, and he'd made it a habit to stay clear of her. Sarka was the most intimidating of the Rowans. He'd heard of the legendary arguments between the siblings along with Sarka's bad tempter.

Cemil began, "Luna, I've been selected to discuss your contract."

At his words, everyone's attention was on the siren.

"I only sang so Charlie wouldn't get away, especially after what he'd done to Cyrus," she said.

"Yes, Myron's cards support your statement." Cemil gave a half smile. "It is why we are willing to overlook the discrepancy. We are grateful to you, really."

The monarch, Sarka, spoke to Luna. "Our brother Cyrus will make a full recovery thanks to you removing the dart before all the poison was injected. Can you tell us what happened?"

Nate listened to Luna's story, realizing he had never even asked her the details. He'd been so relieved she was safe, he could only concentrate on her.

At the end of her recount, Luna asked, "And Charlie? Who is he?"

"That's what we intend to find out. His background check was solid. Whoever hired him covered their tracks." Rekkus prowled closer, and Cemil moved out of the way. Nate didn't like the man's hard expression as he drew closer to Luna. Rekkus added, "I'd like to ask for your full cooperation regarding this investigation."

Sarka handed Rekkus a piece of paper.

Nate leaned forward in his chair, irate. "She's not going to say anything."

Sarka waved her hand in dismissal. "Of course not, it's just legality."

"Nate." Luna placed her palm on his wrist to prevent him from snatching the paper. "I understand.

I'll sign it."

Sarka almost smiled. "On behalf of our family, I want to thank you. You've both done us a service. I highly recommend you two take a walk through the southern forest tomorrow. Spend the whole day if you'd like—"

Rekkus cleared his throat.

Sarka added, "Until you find yourselves famished for dinner."

Tomorrow was their last day full day on the island. With the capture of the assassin, Nate's job was concluded. He was mated to boot. Now all he had to do was convince Luna to return home with him. Her place—under the sea—wasn't a viable option.

Chapter Seven

"Good morning." Sage smiled as Luna cleared the threshold of her room.

Startled, Luna stepped into the corridor, bewildered. "Hello, Sage." She wondered why the willowy, fairy-like woman stood at her door and clutched a tray with two chilled shakes on it. Luna started to close the door behind her, but Nate's fingers caught it from the inside and pried it open.

"Oh, good morning, Sage." He stepped into the hallway and closed the door.

Sage inclined her fair head and presented her tray. "I finally had a chance to bring your shake." She grinned at Luna. "I'm sorry I never got one to you yesterday, but I'm sure you understand." She pointed to the other glass. "And I brought one for your mate as well."

"I'd forgotten all about the shake after what happened yesterday. This is very thoughtful of you to deliver it to my door." Luna accepted the shake and took a long sip. *Did she say, "Your mate"? How did she know?* She supposed it wasn't a lucky guess.

Nate grabbed the pinkish drink and took a sip. "Mmm, raspberry, my favorite."

"I remembered." Sage tucked the empty tray under her arm. "Enjoy the forest. It's an awe-inspiring place...and one of Sarka's favorites." She turned like a ballerina then hummed while she promenaded through the hallway.

The couple called thanks to her retreating form, and Sage waved a hand without turning around.

"I think we are in for a treat, besides these." He held up his smoothie.

***

The trek across the island brought them to the forest by late morning. Vast woodlands were stocked with oak, birch, and cedar trees. Grinning, Luna gazed at her wilderness man, sensing he felt at home in these surroundings. He slipped the backpack strap over his chiseled shoulder and dropped the bag to the ground. He unzipped it, dug around then handed her a bottle of water.

The mighty trees towered and surrounded them, as the plentiful lavender waved around Luna's thighs. After hydrating, Nate took her hand and strolled until he reached a cluster of massive oak trees.

"These are impressive," he said.

Luna released his hand to explore while he continued his inspection. She delighted in finding a small circular pool at their base. Its vibrant teal color surrounded by a heady heather scent drew her immediately. Untying the string at her neck, she shimmied, and her gauzy dress floated to the ground. She stepped away completely naked, having never bothered to buy underwear.

"Let's go in," she squealed, then dropped to the grass and swung her legs in. In a moment, she dropped in to her shoulders. "Ooh, it's deep and warm," she enticed. The temperature didn't matter to her, but she guessed at his preference.

Nate disrobed quickly with a ridiculous grin on his face. He fished something from his shorts' pocket before sauntering over. He dropped in, sloshing the water, and taking up most of the available space. She didn't mind, though.

"I have something for you." He opened his palm, revealing his gift. Two charms winked at her in the sunlight.

"My heart charm," she cried, thinking she'd never see it again after it came loose from her anklet and the cheeky squirrel stole it. "I'm so glad you still have it." But he offered her more. "And what is this other one for?"

"It's a key. You have the key to my heart, Luna."

Nearly a week ago, her soul had been dark, but, since she'd let him in, it seemed the darkness was dissipating. She wanted to show him how much he meant to her. She wanted to make love to him again in the water. Could she pleasure this man and have no desire to sing—no desire to kill? Could her love for her mate truly cure her of her siren's curse? Luna carefully set the charms on a cluster of moss. She swiveled to her mate and moved in to find out how her future would unfold.

Luna and Nate made love in the turquoise pool. To her astonishment and jubilation, the siren's call had ceased.

Luna eventually left the pool to join Nate who had sprawled in the moss to dry. He seemed sated for the time being. She inhaled the woodsy scent, bringing her calmness, content to lie beside him in silence. When Luna got up to slip her dress on so they could continue exploring, she picked out leafy debris clinging to her yard of black hair. She added the charms to her gold anklet while pressing her lips together, hiding her deliriously silly grin. *How did my luck change, mated to this amazing man?* A question tugged at her, and she said, "I've been wondering. How did Sage know we mated?"

"I told Rekkus the night in the Fun Shack when we went up to the bar for drinks how I had found you—that my future mate was my current detail." He tugged his shorts over his hips.

"Hmm...but we hadn't done it yet—*mated*—until later that night."

"Right. But what we did later was more of a final act—a consummation. I knew you were my mate from the moment I saw you. It's kind of a big deal when a true mate is discovered. There's no question Rekkus told the Rowans. Also, on another note, it is why they understood when I fully resigned from the Para Elite reserves." He knelt on one knee to load his shoes and T-shirt into the pack.

"You resigned? Why?" She'd learned he'd had a long career with the Syndicate. They obviously valued him.

Nate, already down on one knee, set the pack aside and reached for her hand. "Well, I was hoping you would come with me to Canada. I have a house in Iqaluit on Frobisher Bay, which opens to the Atlantic

Ocean, so you'd have easy access to the water. I mentioned my sled dog business—I prefer it over soldiering. But, mostly, I have the desire to spend my life with you and make you my wife—in the human sense."

"Like marry me?" she burst out.

He chuckled. "Yes, Luna, will you marry me?"

She stifled her gasp. The symbolic ceremony was a nice touch!

"I hope the charm will do for now, but you can have any ring you want—"

"Yes, Nate, I will marry you!" She fell into his arms to cover him with kisses.

"Luna, my beautiful Luna, I want to hold you in my arms forever."

This man had given her so much in such a short time. She wanted to make him feel the same wild happiness she felt. Leaving his embrace and giving him her most alluring smile, she cooed, "If you catch me, you can do *whatever* you want to me."

Slowly parting his lips, he ground his teeth together. "Run!" he growled, then cloaked.

Luna squealed as she raced off. She dashed behind a massive twisted and knotty tree trunk catching her breath. Noisy, stomping feet alerted her to his presence even though she could see his shimmering form. The ancient Dragon's Blood trees stretched out like an umbrella over her head, allowing the noon sunshine to only penetrate in streams of golden light. The pink-and-red blossoms looked like baby dragons flying and frolicking in the breeze. Never had she run free across the land, with joy and happiness in her heart. It was invigorating.

Their cat-and-mouse chase didn't last long. He uncloaked before her as she skipped around the trees. She screamed with surprise and excitement. Eyes blazing with lust, he cocked a brow asking for one more challenge. But, before she could sprint away, he clasped her thin wrist and jerked her against him. This one motion moistened the apex of her thighs. She placed her fingertips on his hairy chest, itching to run them through the long, dark strands. In one swift move, he had her hands behind her. He held them tight. She was his captive—and she liked it. She sighed, waiting for more. He lowered his head as if to kiss her. She parted her lips in anticipation. But, to her frustration, he teased her by tracing her lips with his tongue. She squirmed, craving for his tongue to do more. Nate's mouth came close to hers again, but he moved lower, kneeling in the grass and pressing hot kisses along her collarbone. While his free hand palmed her breast, pinching at the nub through the thin fabric, his mouth moved to the other breast and nipped. She arched and moaned.

He crouched lower and ducked his head under the hem of her dress, all the while holding her prisoner. He pressed his nose to her inner thigh and inhaled with gusto. She swayed. He followed with one quick lick from her knee to the junction of her legs. Tiny quivers shook her body.

"Mmm, tasty."

"Pleeease, Naaate...ahhh." She wanted him to release his hold. She was dying to touch him—give him pleasure.

He unbuttoned and unzipped his shorts with one hand. When he stood, the fabric pooled at his ankles. Turning Luna around, he released her bound wrists. After he untied the dress strap at her nape, he guided the fabric over the tight points of her breasts and down over her narrow hips until it dropped freely to the ground. He palmed the underside of her breasts and bounced them playfully. He growled in her ear, "I love your tits."

Drawing his palms upward, grazing her pointed nipples, he then crested her shoulders and started down her back, applying pressure and bowing her torso. His knee pushed between her thighs, and she was forced to separate and widen her legs. He held her captive, bent over, as he adjusted his stance preparing to enter her. Luna gathered her hair to one side and twisted to watch him.

He stared at her ass. "You have the most beautiful, tight ass."

She winced as he squeezed it, but she didn't mind because the thirst in his eyes was priceless. She folded over the rest of the way, placing her hands in the grass. He groaned in response to the total access, and lightly brushed his fingers over her—everywhere intimate exposed to him. She shook with tension, waiting for him to enter her.

Finally, he dipped in a finger to test her readiness. She moaned, and her eyelids fluttered closed. He withdrew his wet finger and, a moment later, said, "Mmm, delicious."

She caught her bottom lip between her teeth. He bumped his cock against her smooth ass, prolonging her anticipation. She hung her head in total submission and waited.

When his wide tip filled her opening, she licked her lips. He pressed his cock in farther and farther; he gripped her waist and pressed even farther. She opened her mouth, but no sound came out until he withdrew. She clenched her teeth and sucked air through them. With each stroke, he plunged into her longer and deeper, rocking her forward. She reached up and grasped the nearest and lowest tree branch, curling her fingers around its hard bark. From this position, his momentum was mind-blowing. Luna half-screamed, half-sang as wave after wave of pleasure flooded her. The spasm in her cervix soon rippled throughout her whole body, leaving her trembling. Panting, she tensed under his continued thrusts, riding the swelling of his cock. The sound of his roar sent birds scattering from the treetops. Nate's hand joined hers on the tree branch when he came into her, his hoarse exhale at her ear.

He eased out of her and stepped into the cool grass to stretch his arms over his head. She stood and mimicked his stretching, gratified by the flexing. She grinned as she admired his glossy cock, stretching long in her direction.

"I may need a nap. Come here, beautiful." He led her to a mossy patch, leaving the clothes where they lay. He sprawled against the cushioned ground, and she rested her head in the crook of his arm. "There is no place to better enjoy you than the great outdoors."

"I agree, and, out of the water, I like it when you take me from behind," she admitted.

Nate chuckled, but then said with a serious voice, "Oh, my little siren, I have other ways to make you sing."

***

At the dock, Luna hugged Selena and glanced at the Rowan siblings who had all turned out to wish her and Nate farewell. What pleased her most was that Cyrus was recovered enough to have made the effort.

Luna now had a new, dear friend for life. "Thank you for helping me heal. I promise to return soon. Perhaps for a swim every now and again?"

"I'd love it. Come anytime." Selena held Luna's hands giving them a final squeeze before she let go. "I'll alert the underwater patrol in case you decide to swim ashore again. Rekkus is sure to make some changes since you managed to breach security."

"I'll be adjusting those details right away," Rekkus said as he walked up.

Luna offered him a feeble shrug, but he ignored it. Rekkus didn't seem like the type for lengthy goodbyes.

He confirmed her suspicions when he said curtly to Nate, "Enjoy your retirement and congrats on the engagement." The weretiger strolled away and joined the Rowans.

Luna and Nate boarded the ferry, her fingers tucked into his. Apprehension churned in her as she remembered the last boat she'd sailed on. She had been a prisoner of the tribe with a muzzle around her mouth. She shivered—an unnatural occurrence for a siren. Nate pulled her close, wrapping his arm around her slender shoulders. The latch was secured for departure, and the boat vibrated away from the dock. They waved to their friends, under the deafening blast of the ferry's horn.

Nate moved to a bench seat, the stiff breeze tugging his hair from his handsome face. He gently placed his duffel bag onto the deck and sat. A squeak sounded from within, and she wondered at her new pet. She'd gotten used to catching a glimpse of the squirrel all week, and she forgave the little thief since her charm had been thoughtfully returned. Besides, Nate had sworn the squirrel was responsible for leading him to the cliffs the day he'd found her on the beach with an assassin. *Okay, one tiny squirrel isn't bad.* But then she remembered his dogs. *How am I going to feel about them?* Only time would tell.

He guided her onto his lap until they were nearly nose to nose. The pine-green color of his eyes calmed her.

He brushed a soft kiss on her lips and murmured for her ears only, "I forgot to mention I play guitar and sing a little. When we get home, I want to play you a love song."

"You sing? Oh, Nate, how could you possibly get any better?" She basked in his attention to her every need, gloriously happy.

"Luna, I love you. No one will ever harm you. I will personally see to it. All I wish is to make you happy."

Luna searched the depths of his eyes. In them, she saw intelligence, kindness, and there was the look—the one Selena promised she'd see—like she was the most important person in the world to him. This man loved her and accepted her for who she was.

"Nate, I love you, too. I feel healed of my hatred and sadness. It's in the past, and, now, I look forward to building our future together." She brushed a strand of waving hair from his brow and placed her hands on the soft hair of his jaw. "I feel completely content. I'm ready for a lifetime of happiness with you."

She'd gone to the Wiccan Haus a stranger, a sort of refugee searching for healing and enlightenment. Not only was she healed of her heartache, but the sense of belonging to the *right* someone completed her.

The island disappeared from sight. On the other side of the magical wall of fog, she would start her new journey with Nate.

Two legends.

Siren and Sasquatch.

Together.

Sign up for the Decadent Publishing Newsletter here

http://eepurl.com/SQ75f **and never miss stories like:**

Prologue

An ominous hue shrouded the sliver of red sunset at the western horizon. Dark-gray thunderheads raced across the sky. The rolling clouds and brisk winds against Drake's cheeks promised the arrival of a wicked thunderstorm.

Drake and Levi rode their motorcycles side by side down the highway until they reached the turnoff to the remote industrial area they hadn't visited in years. They rolled up to the parking lot of the decrepit old gym. Drake's palms vibrated from gripping the handlebars for the two-hour drive. He backed up his Triumph and parked alongside his sergeant of arms. They shut down the engines. He pulled his helmet off and hung it on his handlebars then tousled his hair in a bid to loosen it from the dampness against his neck. The stiffness of road lag had settled in his joints. He swung his leg over the seat and stood up to stretch. The ride from Newark to Queens had never been his favorite. Tonight, he'd dreaded it more than ever.

Drake shook his head with a grin. "Old place hasn't changed a bit."

"I wouldn't say that." Levi climbed off his Harley. "It's even more run-down than the last time we were here. Is there any part of this tin shack that isn't rusted?" Thunder rumbled in the distance. "I don't imagine we'll stay any drier inside."

A sudden cascade of icy rain pattered over his leather jacket, drenched his hair, and dripped down his face. Once upon a time, thunderstorms had brought him the greatest pleasure. This one amplified the endless gloom shrouding him.

"Brother...." His best friend grabbed his arm as he reached for the door handle. "Are you sure you wanna do this?"

Torment churned in his gut. "It's not a choice. Sai

needs to know."

Levi patted his shoulder. "Might be easier for me to do it."

He squared his shoulders. "Thanks, buddy. But I'm the VP. I have to own up to this."

"Hey, this is not your fault." Thick strands of soaked black hair dangled from under Levi's red bandana and clung to his face.

Tightness clenched Drake's chest. "Isn't it?" Three hours ago, his guilt intensified after the arrival of the gruesome gift-wrapped box accompanied by a note at the front door. "Sai's gonna have questions for me."

"It's been five years. I don't think there's gonna be a warm welcome party. We're gonna get our asses handed to us."

"Especially after I explain why we're here."

Thunder rolled long and hard throughout the air. Soft cracks of lightning lit up the night sky.

"Let's get this over with." He gripped the cold metal handle and yanked the steel door open. "But keep your eyes open, it's not over by a long shot. I think it's just begun."

The pungent whoosh of residual sweat crept up his nose, and familiar bluesy riffs filled his ears. "Jeff Healey. Smells and sounds the same, too."

Despite the sudden invisible tug in his chest insisting he head to the back office, he resisted. After all this time, a happy reunion would be the last thing to happen tonight. Drake strolled toward the worn and scuffed ring in the center of the mediocre warehouse. The ring he'd spent endless training hours in over years past. The tug alerted him of his target's presence on the premises. It had been ages since he stood here, even longer since he had been welcome to enter the gym uninvited.

Off to Drake's left, weight-lifting sets were lined up alongside the treadmill and boxing bags. Sai's professional days as of late in the mixed martial arts world didn't taint the authenticity of the gym. He glanced up to the cracked black paint of the welcome banner: *Ain't No Rest for the Wicked*. Their gym motto.

The drooping red leather ropes had cracked and faded. Brown splatters of dried blood stained the aged canvas floor, and an inverted milk crate served as a makeshift step into the ring.

"Can I help you?" a distant voice called out. "Unless you're booked in, we're closed, guys. Scheduled sparring only, tonight."

"We're not here to fight," Levi called.

A massive bald guy with dark eyes, light-brown skin, and bulging biceps headed toward to them. He draped a white towel around his thick neck, his gray T-shirt and sweat pants dark with sweat. He sported some impressive bruising and a few gashes on his cheek. No doubt from a gripping champ's training day.

"Oh? How can I help you?"

"We're here to talk to Sai," Drake asserted. "Personal business."

The guy knitted his brows for a moment. "Oh, you mean Viper, right? I'm Hortese, club manager, and you would be?"

"I'm Drake. This here is Levi. We're"—he glanced at his buddy—"family."

The muscle-bound Spanish Inquisition cocked his head to the side and cracked a grin. "Right, thc bikers." He eyed up and down their leather jackets. "Mind if I take a look at your patch?"

Drake nodded. "Sure. Levi?"

Levi turned away, showing the colors on the back of his jacket.

"Mythic Iron. Epic artwork. Love the dragons."

"Thanks." He faced forward again.

Drake covered his mouth to muffle a snicker. "Couldn't help but notice your fresh battle wounds."

He pointed to Hortese's face. "Sai's putting you through blindfold training now?"

The club manager flashed a one-sided grin. "You got it. You've done it, too?"

"We've done our share. Two concussions and a cracked sternum for me."

"Hell yeah," Levi chimed in. "Three broken ribs and a dislocated shoulder."

"So, you're saying I got off easy?" Hortese chuckled.

"For now." Drake pressed his lips tight. "Sai's a ballbuster. You'll get worse, I'm sure, but the champ is convinced it will save your life one day—at least that's what Sai told us after every injury."

"Good to know." The manager shook his hand. "We haven't done any sparring yet. You guys might wanna hang back a bit and let the pent-up aggression deplete before you try and talk to Viper."

Levi curled his lip and snarled, "We'll take our chances. It can't wait. It's important."

Hortese shrugged. "Suit yourselves, it's your funeral." He called out, "Hey, boss, some guys are here to see you."

The grubby office door in the far corner opened with a soft squeak. He stared at the skin-tight, white tank top and baggy nylon Adidas pants. Long black hair, slicked back into a tight ponytail, Sai walked toward them. A scowl contorted her heart-shaped face, her curves still as voluptuous as he remembered. As she approached, she tugged the neckline of her tank top up to hide the vibrant purple dragon's tear marks over her heart.

"I warned you two, if you ever tried to bring me back again, I'd kill you—"

The reminder sent a sharp pain to his scarred shoulder. "Sai," he interrupted her with a stern voice. "That's not why we're here."

The glow of her silver irises darkened as she stepped closer, glaring at him.

She had always been able to see right through his hardened exterior.

"No...." She widened her eyes and shook her head. "I don't want to hear it."

"Babe, please, you have to listen—" Levi asserted.

"I said no!" she hissed. "Hortese, who's scheduled for a bout tonight?" She spun around and jogged over to the banged-up lockers and grabbed a roll of tape.

Levi moved to follow her, but Drake gripped his shoulder. "Don't."

"There are a few new people tonight. Didn't

recognize their names, but they haven't arrived yet," Hortese told Sai.

"Yes we have," a low voice boomed from the doorway.

Drake twisted around to find six, gargantuan men in dark pants and T-shirts, sauntering in. The epitome of bad news with stone-cold expressions, domineering stances, and muscular physiques. Their presence shot pangs of caution through his stomach.

"Brother."

His sergeant of arms mumbled back, "What do you want me to do, take 'em out?"

"Not yet. We don't know why they're here. See how she handles it. We've got her back if anything happens." If only he believed his own words. They had no way to know if these were the same guys who ransacked their clubhouse last night, but he'd bet his patch they were.

"Who's first?" she called out in her raspy, venomous tone.

Drake glanced over to find her narrow her eyes and slowly slither the tip of her tongue across her upper lip. She was pissed, but now she was on guard, too. Sai pounded at the old CD player until the tune "Mortal Combat" blared throughout the gym. Her serpent sense of smell alone would have alerted her to something about the new arrivals he'd already suspected. Her traditional kick-ass tune was the tell. Shit was about to get real.

He moved toward the ring, scanning between her and the encroaching threat. Sai wrapped white tape around her knuckles and hands, tore the end off with her teeth, and tossed the roll on the floor beside her. Her darkened cheeks and narrowed silver eyes revealing her hostility, she hopped up into the ring.

"Hortese, you're done for the night. Go home to your wife. I've got this," she commanded.

"No way." He bolted toward the ring and stopped in front of Drake.

"I said get outta here, now," she seethed.

"Come on, brother, let me," Levi prompted.

"Wait."

"Boss...." Hortese hesitated.

"It's okay. We'll stay," Drake said. "Listen to her. Go home." He let his eyes glow, a small bit of shifting while still controlling the dragon. "We've got this."

Hortese nodded and bolted out of the emergency exit behind the ring.

The familiar internal combustion of heat flared through his veins as his protective mode kicked in.

The six thugs joined them at ringside.

"You guys gonna fight tonight?" the one with a scruffy beard goaded.

"Not if we can help it," Drake offered coolly.

"Sweet, then I'm first, gorgeous." He climbed up into the ring, set one foot forward, and raised his clenched fists. "I've read all about you, lady. Let's dance."

"You're not my type." She held her hands up near her face and braced her bare feet shoulder-width apart. "Bring it."

"Now?" Levi murmured.

"Don't make the first move." In the event of any aggressive movement, Drake was ready to pounce.

"This is gonna be more fun than taking down your old man, bitch," the giant in the ring boasted.

Drake's stomach bottomed out. Sai glanced over to him. She tilted her head in question and he nodded and mouthed, *yeah*.

Now she knew why they had shown up after five years, she glowered at her opponent. Her cheeks blazed red. "Don't count on it—bitch."

The thug launched a fist toward her. She moved to the side and countered with a powerful snap kick to his windpipe. He stumbled forward and gasped, clutching his throat. Before he could tumble to the mat, she catapulted forward and pummeled the thug with rapid strikes to his jaw and nose and knocked him to the ground.

"Get her," he gurgled through bleeding lips.

The guy with a buzz cut moved to climb up into the ring, but Levi booted the milk crate out from under him and pounced on him. A third guy tackled him from behind.

The remaining three guys advanced on Drake. He swung a right hook and clocked the scruffy blond one in the jaw and knocked him down with a single shot. A dark-skinned guy stormed toward him. Drake spun as he crouched with a leg sweep and dropped the guy on his back. He jumped on top of him and bashed in his face until he stopped moving. The last guy tugged at Drake's collar and tried to pull him off his attack. Drake launched a backward fist over his right shoulder, and a loud crack sounded on impact of his knuckles to the guy's face.

The attacker landed on his side, clutching his jaw, and hollered. Blood gushed from his mouth. Drake jumped up and slammed his foot into the attacker's gut then his face. Three strikes and he dropped his arms, his latest attacker out cold.

The first guy he'd knocked down had scrambled to his feet and climbed into the ring where Sai continued to pound on her assailant. A bright glimmer of metal caught the light. The bald guy dove onto her from behind, bowie knife held high. He sliced at her chest and arms with vicious swings. As Drake climbed under the rope, she thrashed about and shoved her attacker back then spun around. Her eyes ablaze with her dragon half, she jumped, landing her legs around his neck. As he continued to slash away at her, she twisted and dropped him to the mat headfirst and knocked him out.

Drake ran to her side and found her skin smoking. "No, Sai, don't do it—" It was too late to stop her. She opened her mouth, her fangs protruded, and she let out a bloodcurdling scream as fiery venom spurted from her teeth. The blazing liquid landed on the battered face of the second invader and set his head on fire.

"Sai," Drake hollered. The other two were out cold on the floor, and Levi was climbing into the ring.

"It's over." Drake wrapped his arms around her from behind, his grip slippery from the blood seeping from her gaping wounds. Tingles radiated through his palms at the touch of her skin. He held on and talked into her ear. "Darlin, you're safe now. I've got you. We've got you. Let the dragon go, please...." He shushed her and held her trembling body.

She fell to her knees and howled, "They killed him. They killed my father...."

Levi moved close and wrapped his arms around them both. "It's okay, baby. We're here now. Let it go, breathe."

Pools of crimson drenched the canvas. Sai went limp, eyes shut, her olive skin white. He pressed the pads of his fingers against the side of her throat. "Her pulse is weak. She's lost a lot of blood." He scooped her up into his arms, and Levi helped him get her out of the ring.

Panic had taken hold, but, as she lay unconscious, an eerie calm washed over him. If they didn't think fast and do something, she'd bleed to death. "Grab the first aid kit, on the wall over there," he barked.

Before the words finished leaving his mouth, his partner raced over and grabbed the rusted metal box. Lucky they kept it in the same place.

"The bastard got her pretty good." Levi set the box on the ground and held Sai up by the shoulders as Drake wrapped gauze around her chest and tied it off.

Swift and precise, he secured the bandages and

moved on to her arms and thighs. "We need to call for cleanup." Six bodies lay on the floor. The guy whose jaw Drake had shattered started to groan and move.

"I got this." Levi stood up and let out a growl.

"Don't kill him until we get some answers," he ordered.

"Right." Levi nodded. "Once I get him squared away, I'll get the guys to bring Doc to patch her up...and a cleanup crew for the rest."

Levi bolted over to the target and slammed his foot into his gut before he hauled him up into the air by the collar.

"I mean it, alive for answers," Drake warned.

Sai was unconscious and pale from blood loss, her tank top sliced open, along with her flesh. The gash ran six inches from her collarbone toward her heart, stopping short of her purple teardrops.

"Doc will fix you up, good as new, darlin'." He brushed her blood-soaked hair back from her face.

A long-time member of the MC, Doc patched everyone up after fights and bike accidents. Hell, he'd stitched up Drake and Levi the night she stabbed them both.

"Good as new...."

Part of him didn't believe his words, but he

couldn't lose her, not again, not like this. He pulled his leather jacket off and draped it over her battered body. Drake lifted his mate into his arms and rocked her. How could he fail again? First, Gin, her mother then Omar, her father and his MC President, and now he failed to protect her. He yanked his cell phone out of his coat pocket and speed-dialed thirty three.

"Kane, it's Drake. I need your help."